TALES
FROM THE
FLESH ORACLE

Sean Southerland-Kirby

Tales from the Flesh Oracle

For Mozz and Julie
Thank you for your support
and for believing in me

(Even though I know this
isn't your cup of tea)

STORY ONE

The Flesh Oracle

Hawthorne blossom swept across the bonnet of the Ford Anglia. A spring breeze sent the delicate white petals dancing in swirls across the chipped and faded maroon paint. Father Caleb Kedge collected papers from the passenger foot-well as the car lurched in a tilt towards the drivers side.

"Are you sure you don't need a hand?" he said, turning to realise the window was still closed. Winding it down, he stuck his head out to see his mentor Father Eskil crouched by the back wheel. With his sleeves rolled up he turned the crank of the jack wedged below the car. "Do you need any help Mark?" The older man looked up briefly, sweat beading his brow as he strained for the last few turns.

"No... it's... nearly.... done!" - the last word becoming more of a hefty sigh as he stood up - "Just make sure those papers are in order before we set off again."

"Of course, Father." Caleb diverted his gaze away from the gruesome images accompanying several documents and instead watched the older mans reflection in the cracked wing mirror. Father Eskil may have been in his fifties but Caleb still had pangs of lust for him. The church hadn't rid him of them as he had hoped. In time, though, he had learnt to quash his urges. Seeing the black shirt cling to his muscular sweaty body was a trial unto itself for the young man. Taking a deep breath and clutching at the cross he wore, he sent a silent prayer of strength to the Virgin Mary and got back to his task. "I told you we should have asked for a new car. This old rust bucket is a death trap." He rapped his knuckles on the plastic dashboard.

"Just because something is old, doesn't mean it's worthless." Father Eskil had removed all the bolts from the blown out tyre and was just about to switch for the spare. "Come now Caleb, it's not our place to question the diocese on the provisions they have for us. The car is fine, even if it is as old as Methuselah," he laughed, slipping the last bolt into place and tightening it down. He put the damaged tyre into the boot and walked along the passenger side, "Besides, it ended up being a fortuitous turn." He opened the passenger door and looked down at Caleb's furrowed brow. "It's your turn to drive." He extended a hand to help the younger man out of the car and took his place in the passenger seat. Shaking his head and laughing, Caleb jogged round to the drivers side and soon enough they were off down the country lane.

"I have to warn you." Father Eskil thumbed through pages in a manila folder as they entered a tunnel of tree cover. "This wont be like Ruislip."

"I know Father. I've read the files."

"There's a big difference between reading a file and

actually facing a patient. This is not just another bored housewife hearing voices, or a grieving child afraid of the dark and making up boogie men. These people are locked away for a reason." Closing the file with a sigh, he rubbed the bridge of his nose.

"Then why send us in at all? I mean, surely the doctors have diagnosed some mental health issue that would explain away a possession."

"Its not always as easy as that Caleb. Think of our first few cases together. You would have been convinced too if I hadn't shown you the tricks these people use." Caleb nodded. In 35 investigations together, they had yet to confirm a single legitimate case of possession.

"Is that why you've been so on edge about this one? Because we're going to a mental hospital?"

"Good grief no!" Mark laughed, "my mother was a nurse in an asylum when I was a much younger man. It was through her that I met Doctor Wiley." He gave Caleb a sideways look as they exited the leafy tunnel and entered sunlight.

"Hold on, you know Doctor Wiley? The same Doctor Wiley who put in this request for an investigation?"

"The very same," Mark let out a long breath. "He knew me as I came out of seminary. Already a brilliant doctor, he sought my advice on 'spiritual matters'. He was convinced that the human mind had the potential to tap into things beyond our own senses. My mother had told him of my calling towards the rites of exorcism and he reached out to me. Asked if he could attend and witness as a medical professional. Became a sort of team. Then, after several years working together, he wrote and published a pseudo-scientific journal. Of course he changed all the names, including mine, but he had released it without mine or the church's permission. He was barred from attending rites or from future publications pertaining to Vatican approved exorcisms. He moved out here to Wales and set up a private practice, which grew into the facility we're on our way to now."

"How long has it been since you last saw him?"

"More than 20 years now. We tried to stay in contact afterwards. We grew apart though. He was too focused on his work and I on mine. In his last letter to me he said 'faith should be left to the incurious mind while science moves understanding forward.' It was clear to me then we had diverged too far apart. His research has yielded great advances in psychology and psychiatry though. There's no doubting he is a brilliant man."

"No wonder you are anxious then, given your history. How much longer is it anyway?" Caleb glanced at his watch. Dusk would be setting in soon and he hated driving in the dark, especially on rural roads with no street lights.

"About an hour. I'll flick through these files again and let you drive."

It was close to two hours later that the priests drove up to the iron gates of the hospital. Gas lamps either side of the gate protruded from ivy-clad brick pillars. The flickering light created shifting shadows of the surrounding walls. More ivy had grown through the iron bars and the red brick posts that made up the perimeter. On the left, the leaves had been trimmed back away from a worn but polished sign. The words 'Topher Shades Sanatorium' reflected the gaslights.

"Get out and see if there's a bell or buzzer will you. I'll put these away." Mark was putting the files into a briefcase on his lap. Caleb got out and, after stretching his legs and back, walked over to inspect the gate. He couldn't see a button or intercom. There didn't even appear to be a knocker of any sort.

"Well? What's taking so long?" Father Eskil had wound down his window and looked impatient.

"I can't find anything to let them know we're here. Why don't you honk the horn a few times. That should get someones attention."

"I don't think that would be a good idea." Caleb jumped out of his skin and turned to face the man who had spoken. The small, tweed-clad man struck a flame on a gold cigarette lighter and used it to light the lantern he was carrying. "I do apologise young man, I hope I didn't scare you too much. You look like you've seen a ghost." - the words of concern didn't quite mask the pleasure in the mans voice at having scared someone so thoroughly - "Doctor Whiley." He extended a loose-skinned hand through the bars.

"Father Kedge," he shook the extended hand. "You did take me by surprise I admit," he laughed, clutching his chest, "I believe you know my colleague, Father Eskil." Mark was already out of the car and walking over to the two men.

"Hello Felix. Long time."

"Indeed it is." Both men stared at each other for a moment then simultaneously broke into smiles, "It's good to see you old friend! Let me get this gate open and welcome you in properly." He stuck a large rusted key into the lock of the towering iron gates. Several other ancient looking keys jangled on the ring they shared as the gates swung in. "There we are! Just follow the road up to the side of the house and you can park; there are plenty of spaces. I'll cut across the lawn and meet you at the front door." He waited for the car to cross the threshold then locked up and headed towards the building on the hill. The Ford Anglia protested slightly at the incline up to the sanatorium.

"Well it's as big as I imagined for a private hospital. Creepy too." Caleb shuddered a little at the thought of Hammer horror spectres and spooks walking the halls.

"Don't get yourself too excited. I just hope the rooms are warm; converted manor houses always run the risk of a cold night's sleep. From what I understand, though, this is a state-of-the-art facility so we're in good hands, I'm sure." They parked the Anglia in a small car park; its headlights swallowed by a privet border as they inched forwards into a space. There were enough spaces for thirty or more cars but less than half a dozen were occupied. Their polished shoes crunched the pea gravel as they made their way to the front of the building. Caleb had the car keys dangling from his mouth, both men having their hands full with a briefcase and travel bag each. They inspected the building as they walked and noticed that only a handful of the barred windows were lit; their limited light shining down on glimpses of manicured lawns and tasteful topiary bushes. They rounded the corner and found Doctor Whiley stood by the front doors at the top of a sweeping stone staircase. The top and bottom were marked each side with more of the topiaries, these ones potted. The doctor wasn't alone. Standing in the ring of light afforded by the lantern was a potato sack of a man and a plain faced Amazonian woman. Both wore private security uniforms. The lumpy man lumbered down the stairs, huffing and puffing with each step, to meet the priests.

"The doctor has asked that I take your bags to your rooms," he said, his tone friendly, with an undeniably London accent. He took both bags on one hand, leaving them their briefcases. "I'm Gary" - he flicked the corner of the plastic name badge - "my associate up there with the good doctor is Marcy. She don't talk much but she's built like a bull with a temper to match," he laughed to himself as they started up the stairs. "I'll make sure these are in your rooms before you get there."

"Thank you Gary." Caleb wiped the spittle from the corner of his mouth and put the soggy leather keyring and car key in to his pocket.

"You picked a nice time for a visit, all things considered. Its been lovely sunshine the last few days." He waddled up the stairs with the priests a step behind. "Though I suppose you'll be too busy to enjoy it what with, well you know, the reason you're 'ere."

"Yes that's quite enough of that," warned Felix, "just see those bags get to each room and get back to your post. Marcy will relieve you once she's let us through the security gates."

"Yes boss." Marcy opened the front doors and everyone followed her into the spacious hall. "Don't be too long Marcy, I'm gagging for a ciggie. Bloody skeleton rota, never getting a break..." the words trailed off in a murmured echo as he wandered off on his task. Mark gave a whistle of appreciation at the room they found themselves in. Unlike the Gothic exterior, the interior was sparkling white. The floors were white marble with inlaid borders and a similar border ran along the white walls at waist height. A few plush chairs and a reception desk in the middle of the room were the only pieces of furniture; the polished dark wood and green leather reflecting the bright neon light overhead. The reception computer was switched off and the ficus beside the desk looked to be in need a good watering Marcy locked the front doors and, with a tilt of the head and rolling eyes, had everyone follow her. They headed left in the opposite direction to Gary. All four hallways leading off the central entryway had a double set of sturdy metal bars part way down, each with a sliding metal door; it gave the effect of an air lock.

"We just need to check you through security, you understand," Felix explained, bringing up the rear of the group, "Gary will check your bags before leaving them in your rooms. I hope you don't mind?"

"Not at all, we quite understand," Caleb said. Their footsteps echoed as they walked.

"This is the administration wing. Its just a collection of offices really, hardly a wing. But one must keep up the pretence in a building like this. Security office just doesn't have the same grandeur as administration wing." Marcy had unlocked the first gate, and sliding the door aside, stood like a sentinel till all three men had passed her. She locked the door behind her and proceeded to the second gate, going through the same process. Unlock, escort, lock.

"You look a little worried, Father Kedge." Felix noted.

"I've just never been inside somewhere with such strict security. It's a little unnerving." His voice quivered a little. "And please, Caleb is fine."

"Then you must call me Felix. Although that's just in private, you understand," correcting himself with a finger in the air. "In front of the patient I am Doctor and you will both be Father. Agreed?"

"Of course!" agreed Mark.

"Excellent." Felix clapped both of the men on their backs as they walked. They passed a few closed and plain doors before Marcy stopped at a windowed door and unlocked it. She turned on the lights of the security office and sat behind one of the several cheap desks on a much too small swivel chair that protested with a creak of cheap plastic. Felix carried on talking while Marcy got together some forms, separated them in to two piles and fastened them to clipboards. "Of course the security measures are more about keeping the world out than keeping patients in. Their safety is our top priority you understand."

"Sit!" interrupted Marcy, in monotone. Mark and Caleb each took a seat opposite her. Marcy didn't look up. "Name?" the monotone accompanied a pen pointed at Mark.

"Father Mark Eskil." She scribbled on the form.

"Age?"

"54." Another scribble. She switched to another clipboard and form.

"Name?" This time the monotone and pen directed at Caleb.

"Father Caleb Kedge." Scribble.

"Age?"

"25". Scribble.

"Take these. Fill in the rest." She handed them their respective forms and took a pen each for them from a 'Best Aunt' mug on her desk. "Cases please." She took the two briefcases from them and flicked carefully through the papers they had, inspecting the contents carefully. After a few minutes, she nodded an okay to Felix, closed the cases and handed them back. She took both clipboards back and took a hand held metal detector from her desk drawer. "Stand!" She pointed at Mark with the detector. She ran it over his body and whenever machine squealed he showed keys, coins, cross, whatever was being picked up by the wailing device. Caleb did the same when he was asked. Again she nodded at Felix and put the detector back in its drawer. She stood in front of the two men and presented a plastic wrapped cylinder. "Hobnob?" She offered the biscuits unwrapping the folded over top of the packet.

"Oh thank you, that would be lovely." Caleb took two, nibbling on one and putting the other in his pocket. "For later." He grinned. She swung the packet round to Mark.

"Not for me thanks. I'm more of a Garibaldi man you understand." He winked at Marcy. For the first time since they'd met she smiled, if only for the briefest moment.

"Well then, now that's all settled, shall we head to my library for a drink?" suggested Felix.

Several security gates later and they were settled in the opulent surrounding of the doctor's library. Marcy had left them at the final gate with a nod and went to relieve Gary so that he could enjoy his smoke. "Do you still take your brandy over ice Mark?" Doctor Whiley stood at the open globe, ice tongs in hand.

"I do indeed. Some things never change." He was starting to relax in to the large leather recliner. The company of his old friend and the smell of old books relaxed him after the long drive.

"Quite right." Felix pincered cubes from the bucket seated amid the bottles in the globe and filled the glasses on a silver tray by his side. "And for you Caleb? Brandy?"

"I'm afraid I don't imbibe," he held a hand up in apology, "but if you have a coke?"

"Not a problem. One cola drink for the young man." He picked out a can and closed the globe. Between the three matching seats was a table, onto which the doctor placed the tray. He struck a long match from a caddy on the mantle and lit the gas fireplace. He took his seat between the two priests, facing the flames. "You don't mind my smoking I hope?" Reaching into his inner jacket pocket he retrieved a gold case with several long, slender cigars which he offered to the other men. They declined. He shrugged and lit one. "The older one gets, the simpler life's pleasures are. Don't you agree?" he chuckled, "maybe I should have been a philosopher and I wouldn't have to deal with this damnable place." He sighed heavily, looking every one of his 63 years. He took a large swig of brandy.

"The alleged possession you mean?" Caleb asked, cracking the can open and taking a fizzy sip.

"Possessions," corrected Felix, "whether they are alleged or real is down to your investigation, is it not?"

"Two separate cases in the same place is exceedingly rare. But there is precedence," noted Mark. "I'm afraid the paperwork from the diocese was limited. I understand that there have been several deaths connected to the case? Why haven't the police been involved?" Felix took a long pull on his cigar, the glowing red tip throwing his wrinkles into sharper relief.

"The first few deaths were all deemed natural causes. Then there was the suicide of the first patient I suspect of possession. That's when the police got involved. Thankfully I have assisted the police many times in the past so I am afforded some leeway you understand. After the suicide verdict was declared, I decided to reduce patient numbers from twelve to just one and cut down staff hours."

"Had there been any interaction between the patients?" Mark had taken a notebook from his pocket and was making notes.

"That's one of the peculiar things. They had both been in different wards, isolated from each other. Luther, the first patient, was admitted for violent behaviour and hallucinations. Reece, the second, had an eating disorder and was a private patient. Luther had been in solitary confinement. They would never have crossed paths."

"Had?" Caleb sat forwards, eyebrow cocked.

"Hm?" Felix blew smoke from his nose.

"You said 'had'. Reece 'had' an eating disorder."

"What a smart young man." Felix gave an appreciative smile before his face became somber again. "I'm afraid Reece also passed away recently. I believe..." He was cut short by an unexpected tear. He wiped it away with a purple pocket square.

"What on earth is the matter Felix?" Mark had never

seen Felix emotional and so sat forward to place a comforting hand on his old friends knee.

"I believe that whatever this entity is, it has found another host to inhabit. A third victim. I asked for you by name, Mark. I have no one else to turn to who would understand" - he was visibly sobbing now - "Mark it's my granddaughter, Lydia." He clutched at the priest's hand, his eyes pleading for help. For a moment, Mark couldn't respond. Long buried images, creeping forwards in his mind, gave him pause. He pushed them back.

"Of course we'll help," he said.

"Absolutely," chimed in Caleb, "Whatever you need."

"I rather think I've made an old fool of myself." Felix half laughed and with a final wipe of this eyes stuffed the pocket square back into his jacket. "It has been a long day for us all and I think I'm getting ahead of myself. Let us rest and after breakfast tomorrow we can start at the beginning. I will help you in anyway I can with the investigation."

"That's sounds like an excellent plan," Mark patted Felix's knee before sitting back to finish his brandy in a large swallow.

"This wing of the building is a completely secure guest wing. Only the bedrooms and my office have locks. There is a small kitchen and dining room and of course this library. Feel free to use them as you wish. I feel I should retire to bed. Your rooms are at the other end of the corridor." He took two keys from his pocket, each one attached to a plastic keyring with a number, and put them on the table. "There are no other guests so you wont be disturbed. I'll see you in the morning." Felix left them both in the library enjoying the fire. Several minutes of silence passed as Mark studied the blue tinted flickering flames of the fireplace. The spell was broken by Caleb.

"Should we call the diocese and tell them about the doctor's granddaughter? Seems a bit odd that they weren't informed, doesn't it?"

"Its not a problem. We'll carry out the investigation as normal. I trust Felix. He must have a good reason for omitting some of the information. Lets rest and pray the morning brings more answers." They switched off the gas fire and made their way down the corridor to their rooms. They had been set up in adjoining rooms at the end of the hall; mirrors of each other. Each room was comfortably appointed with a large bed, desk and chair, wardrobe and chest of drawers. Each also had an en-suite shower room. Their bags had been placed on their respective beds. They were so weary after travelling that neither could be bothered unpacked their belongings. Instead, they opted to pray and sleep.

Caleb woke to the sound of someone whistling a merry tune as the early morning sun sent shards of light through the barred window and across his face. He got up groggily and put on a dressing gown and slippers he'd spied in the wardrobe before getting into bed last night. He caught sight of himself in the mirror on the dresser and tried unsuccessfully to flatten the cow lick on the right side of his head. He left his room and followed the sound of the whistling down the hall. Just past the library was another door. It was open and the smell of bacon wafted out in to the sterile hospital air. He poked his head in to the room.

"Hello?" The small kitchen was a whirlwind of steam, pots and pans. At its centre stood a small round woman in a blue hairnet and stained apron.

"Jesus Christ!" she jumped round in fright to face Caleb, "I'm so sorry." A mortified look crossing her face. "I can't believe I just took the Lord's name in vain, and in front of a man of the cloth no less. My father would be mortified. My god, what's wrong with me? See, there I go again! Please sit down father and let me fix you breakfast." She had left the stove and was pulling out a chair at one of the three tables in the room. "Can I get you a tea? Coffee? Juice? What would you like?"

"Tea, please," he said with a giggle as he took a seat, "And don't worry about taking the Lord's name it vain. I won't tell if you don't." He gave her a wink.

"You're a kind man. Although I suppose you have to be. Bless you anyway. Wait, can I do that, or is blessing your thing? Sugar?" she was poised with a teaspoon over the sugar bowl as the kettle rumbled to a boil.

"None for me thanks. I'm sweet enough already. And I'll take any and all blessings offered." They both laughed.

"I was so happy to hear you were coming for poor Lydia. She's a lovely girl, all things considered. Plus with all the patients sent home and staff hours cut down, I've had no one to cook for, save Doctor Whiley, and he's hardly one for a large meal. I swear that man would choose bran flakes over a roast dinner." She brought over a yellow mug filled with tea; blue letters on its side explaining that 'You don't have to mad to work here, but it helps'. Caleb thought that this might not be in the best taste considering their location, but didn't mention it.

"Now, I'm making a proper cooked breakfast and I'll hear no complaints on the matter. Christ it feels good to cook something proper. Sorry father, excuse me again. Now the only question is, how would you like your eggs? Scrambled, scrambled or scrambled?" she winked at him, grinning widely at her own joke.

"Scrambled will be lovely, thank you."

"Good morning." Mark had found them although he looked like he'd been awake a good portion of the night.

"Good morning," Caleb greeted him, "You look a little worse for wear. Bad night's sleep?"

"You could say that," he stretched out his back and yawned.

"I'm not surprised," chimed in hairnet, "The mattresses here aren't the most comfortable."

"Oh Mark this is..." realisation struck home. "I'm sorry my dear, I didn't actually catch your name."

"Not to worry. I'm Polly Wheeler. You can call me Peaches, everyone does. You join your friend and I'll make you a drink. Tea, coffee or juice?"

"Coffee, please. Thank you. Black, three sugars." Mark took a seat opposite Caleb.

"Now as I told your colleague here. I'm making a proper cooked breakfast and I'll hear no complaints on the matter. Now the only question is, how would you like your eggs? Scrambled, scrambled or scrambled?" She winked again, grinning wider at her joke the second time. Caleb rolled his eyes out of sight of her.

"Scrambled then," he told her in an uninterested tone, looking down at his fingernails.

"Of course father." Her face sank as she went over again

to the stove.

"You really didn't sleep well. No one could accuse you of being a morning person." Caleb nodded his head toward Peaches. Mark sighed.

"I guess middle-age and cheap mattresses don't mix." He was neither awake enough yet nor in the mood to start discussing the dreams that had been keeping him awake through the night. "Peaches, please forgive me. I assure you I'm a much nicer man when I've had a decent sleep." He smiled warmly at her and she softened in to her own smile.

"Well I suppose I can't hold it against a man of God. Besides, I'm just the same if I haven't slept. My husband, God rest his soul, used to say to me, 'Peaches' he'd say 'go and have a nap before you really offend someone'. He was always so clever about that kind of stuff. Now I've got red sauce, brown sauce, mustard or mayonnaise." She took the selection of condiments from a hostess trolley she'd wheeled over and put them in the middle of the table. "Can't see the point of mayonnaise on a full English personally. Much too French. But the choice is there if you want it." She then took the two plates from the trolley and placed one in front of each of them. "And here's your coffee too." She placed down the mug. "Anything else you need, just ask, I'll just be over here washing up these pots and pans."

"Thank you Peaches. It all looks delicious." Mark looked down at the greasy pile of food and his stomach lurched a little. 'I can't be hung over after a single brandy' he thought. 'Maybe I'm coming down with something.'

"Yes thank you," said Caleb, full of appreciation as he

squirted a large blob of ketchup between the mushrooms and hash browns. Caleb said grace for the two of them and got stuck in. Mark tentatively ate a few pieces then gingerly nibbled a piece of toast while he sipped his slightly burnt coffee.

"If you don't want those sausages..." Caleb's voice broke the unpleasant train of thoughts Mark was on.

"You go ahead." He slid the plate over the Caleb. He had never understood how this young man could eat so much junk and still be so slim. Hollow legs he thought. They finished up and thanked Peaches before heading back to their rooms to shower, shave and dress ready for the day. Mark was lost, looking at his haggard face in the mirror of the dresser, when a small knock came at his door. The lumpy security guard was standing in the corridor.

"When you're ready Father, Doctor Whiley has asked me to escort you both to the staff meeting room in the main hospital. Father Kedge said he'll just be a minute."

"Thank you um, Gary wasn't it?"

"That's right father." He smiled brightly back at the priest.

"I'll just be a moment too." Mark closed the door. He took a smaller bag from his travel bag, and after adjusting his dog collar, tucked the small bag under his arm and picked up the briefcase of files. He opened the door to find Caleb and Gary merrily chatting and laughing.

"You look a bit more like yourself. Ready to go?" asked Caleb.

"As ever. Lead the way Gary." They followed him down several corridors and through security gates. A few

minutes later they were in a corridor that smelled heavily
of disinfectant. A rack of empty pigeon holes, each
labelled for a different doctor, stood to one side, all but
one being empty. Dr Whiley's section was full of
paperwork. The rest of the corridor had the usual
trappings of a staff-only area. Posters reminding people to
wash their hands or to 'be aware whilst in open patient
areas' were secured to the walls with clumps of blu-tack.
A cork board had several notices pinned to it. A passive
aggressive statement caught Mark's eye as they passed; a
notice from a Helena about only eating food you have
brought in yourself and yes that includes strawberry
muller corners which were clearly labelled. Mark smirked
at the pettiness of office politics.

"It's the second door on the right there," pointed potato-
sack Gary. "I'll leave you to it then I suppose. If you ever
need us, just use one of the intercom buzzers." He pointed
to a big red button with a speaker grill underneath.
"They're dotted around all over in the corridors." The
radio at his belt beeped loudly just then. He put the box to
his face and pressed the button on its side. "I'll be right
down Marcy." Struggling to reattach the clip to his belt, he
put the radio in his pocket instead and excused himself,
leaving the two priests in the corridor. Doctor Whiley's
head, like a tortoise's from its shell, appeared from the
doorway to greet them.

"Good morning gentlemen. Come come, I'm just about
set up in here." The blinds had all been pulled down in
the room and the lights turned off. At the front right of the
room stood Doctor Whiley at a lectern. "I hope you don't
mind the setup. I'm just so used to giving lectures, it

seems only natural to me." He clicked a button in his hand and the projected white square behind him launched into a power-point presentation. "Please take a seat wherever you'd like and feel free to ask any questions." The tables in the room were arranged in a three rows. They both sat on the middle row in the centre. Mark took out a notebook and pen while Caleb settled back in his chair. The screen read 'Confidential' in large red letters. Below in smaller black text 'The information you are about to view is of a private nature. Please treat these cases with the strictest confidence.' Doctor Whiley pointed at the disclaimer with a telescoping pointer. "You have both agreed to these terms when you signed your security forms. Do you still agree?"

"Of course," Mark waved impatiently.

"Agreed," Caleb nodded.

"Excellent, then let us begin." Doctor Whiley clicked the button in his hand and the text transitioned to the picture of a rough looking bald man. "Luther Brown. 32. Caucasian. six feet tall. Luther came to us via the criminal justice system. A confirmed neo-Nazi, he was heavily involved with a white supremacist group. Serving a double life sentence for the murder of both his brother and his brother's wife. He apparently didn't agree with their marriage, she being an African girl. You may remember the case from several years ago. It was national news for quite some time." The screen now displayed several newspaper clippings and stills of TV news reports from the time.

"I remember this" - Caleb sat forwards in his chair - "When the police arrived at the house he was drinking coffee at the kitchen table. He'd sat the decapitated bodies at the table too with their heads in their laps."

"Exactly right" - Doctor Whiley pointed at Caleb with the telescopic pointer - "He showed no remorse at his trial and was demonstrated to be in full possession of his faculties. A violent sociopath by clinical definition. Whilst in prison, he became a member of a gang of like-minded racists. The usual kind of prison gang structure that happens, you understand. A couple of months ago, he was found in the work out room of the prison covered in blood. Three members of his own gang had been brutally bludgeoned to death with a dumbbell." The next few slides were of the smashed corpses. Mark grimaced. "Luther was in a state of shock for several days with no memory of what happened. Prison footage however clearly shows him committing the murders." The button clicked and the screen came to life. Grainy black and white footage of an ill equipped gym flickered as four men worked out. Suddenly one of them, Luther, jumped up as if struck by lightning and proceeded to quickly smash the skulls of the other three men. Then quietly and calmly he sat in the corner of the room and picked brain matter off his prison uniform as he waited for guards to bust in. When they did, one vomited as Luther turned to look into the security camera and smile, his eyes reflecting light briefly and making Mark squirm in his seat as the footage paused. Caleb looked a shade paler even in the dim room. "I apologise gentlemen. I should have warned you there would be video." Doctor Whiley clicked again and another picture of Luther appeared, this time dressed in patient garb. His eyes sunk back into blackened sockets, his cheek bones pronounced under gaunt skin, several bruises across his head and face. He looked almost unrecognisable. "This was taken just three weeks later on his admittance here. The prison medics were unable to make him eat much more than bread and water, he hardly slept and he kept repeating that the devil made him do it."

"Sounds like someone wanted an insanity plea," said Caleb.

"That doesn't make sense," countered Mark, "Why would someone serving double life, who showed no remorse for the murder of his own family member, suddenly want an insanity plea for murdering three fellow convicts? It doesn't add up."

"Exactly my point Mark. I'm glad we're on the same page," Doctor Whiley tipped a nod to his old friend. "When Luther was admitted I was away in Cambridge visiting Lydia. A colleague, Doctor Singh performed the interview you're about to see." The next click brought up footage of Luther strapped to a chair and facing someone off camera. A female voice came from off screen.

"Mr Brown. Do you know where you are?"

"Hospital."

"Good Mr Brown. Do you know what kind of hospital?"

"A mental one." He looked down at his lap.

"Not quite the words we like to use, but correct. Do you understand why you are here?" An incomprehensible murmur started to come from Luther. "Mr Brown? Luther? Do you understa-"

"I DIDN'T DO IT!" Luther's shout cut her short. The muscles in his neck were strained and red. He started rocking and thrashing from side to side in the chair, making it slide and squeal on the marble floor. "It wasn't me, they made me do it, the devil did it, the devil made me do it." He repeated the mantra over and over and over.

"There is no such thing as the Devil, Mr Brown," Doctor Singh's calming voice cut through. Luther stopped suddenly and slowly raised his head to look at the doctor seated off-screen. His face contorted into a monstrous, lip-cracking grin, his eyes reflected light again briefly as he turned his face to her. He opened his mouth and screamed, the wretched noise shifted to below human pitch. The voice seemed to come from all around the room as it reverberated, before breaking into a cackle. His deranged eyes fixed on doctor Singh.

"Dæmonia vorabit vos," the growling voice said before Luther started convulsing and the video footage stopped.

"Demons eat you?" Caleb asked his mentor in a hushed voice.

"Something like that," Mark said, scribbling in his notebook. "Demons will devour, consume, eat. The translation isn't exact, but it's something along those lines. I don't suppose Luther had any reason to know Latin?" He asked Doctor Whiley.

"None that I could unearth."

"Well it is what it is," Mark said non-committally, "Please continue Felix."

"Certainly. Luther was placed in a maximum security cell for the safety of all concerned. Upon my return a week later, I received a full report from Doctor Singh. She was insistent that she be the one to continue his treatment. I was assured that she would always have a guard with her and security protocols would be in place. That seemed perfectly reasonable to me, considering the patient. Besides, Doctor Singh was a valued colleague and I trusted her judgement. Not to mention that with Lydia's research trip completed and her imminent arrival here, I had my hands full. Doctor Singh gave me daily updates and it's only as I reflect back now that I can say she looked more and more tired as the days went on. It was about that time of course that I found out about the guard's death. Doctor Singh had kept her word and had been taking a guard into each session. That is until the guard suffered a fatal heart attack at only 36 years old. Doctor Singh continued sessions for several days without replacing her attendant guard. She had started to show signs of obsession with Luther. Well of course, when I found out I ordered her to take a leave of absence and I took over the treatment myself. She didn't take the leave willingly. She would phone all hours of the day and night to check on him. Our poor receptionist Jackie bore the brunt of her incessant calls while I took up the challenge of Luther's treatment."

"I suspect such an abrupt change of doctor didn't go down too well with Luther?" Caleb asked.

"Actually it was quite the reverse. On our first session I entered the room and sat across the table from the restrained man and set my tape recorder to record the session. I had a guard just outside the door naturally." Doctor Whiley clicked again and the click-whir of the tape recorder filled the room.

"Good afternoon Luther, my name is Doctor Wh…"

"We know who you are Doctor Whiley. Such a shame Doctor Singh can't join us. We were enjoying her." Several voices laughed in unison. "Do send our regards."

"Impressive trick with the voices Luther." No one spoke for a moment, then the voice of a young girl started to speak.

"Doctor Whiley, fix your head. If he can't, you'll be dead," came the voice, singing in a school yard fashion, followed by someone whistling three drawn out notes. Its eerie, tuneless cadence sending a chill up the spine of both priests; Mark looked ashen.

"Are you alright?" Caleb put a hand on his mentor's shoulder.

"Fine," he said, shaking his head a little and making more scribbles in his notebook.

"You can understand why I felt uncomfortable around the man," Doctor Whiley said looking at Mark. Caleb turned back to the doctor.

"I think anyone would. Although we have heard voices like this before. I've been both amazed and terrified by some of the things we've heard." Unconsciously Caleb crossed himself and kissed his rosary.

"As have I, dear boy." Doctor Whiley smiled at the young man. "This is not my first time at the rodeo you might say. Isn't that right Mark?" Mark had managed to compose himself and nodded at the doctor.

"Felix knows not to take things at face value, no matter how disturbing. How did he respond to your treatment?"

"It was tough and short lived I'm afraid. I have several more recordings of different voices and that same tuneless whistle, but ultimately our treatment sessions only lasted 5 days, the last being the 23rd. A day I wish I could forget."

"What exactly happened?" asked Mark.

"That morning, Jackie the receptionist came to see me directly to discuss the phone calls she had been receiving from Doctor Singh's home phone number. Most asking about Luther, how he was, had he asked about her. That sort of thing. But several had come through of horrific screams from several voices. She'd even had a couple which were nothing more than someone whistling down the line. She was unnerved by the calls and had been having nightmares as a result of them and kindly asked me to speak to Doctor Singh on her behalf. I assured her I would visit Doctor Singh as soon as I was able. That afternoon I had decided to start unpacking some of Lydia's expedition artifacts and files. No more than 90 minutes later and an orderly came to fetch me. I followed them to the reception to find a blanket draped over a form at the desk. I knew from the shape it could only be a body in the chair. Sure enough, under the blanket was Jackie. Her face a mask of distress and her hand, white knuckled around the receiver of the phone. My worst fears confirmed when I checked the caller display. Doctor Singh was the last caller. Later autopsy revealed Jackie passed of a brain haemorrhage. I had no option but to ask the police to call on Doctor Singh."

"How old was Jackie?" asked Caleb.

"25. Her whole life ahead of her and taken in a flash." Doctor Whiley looked forlornly at the floor before sighing, taking a deep breath and continuing, "By the time it came to Luther's session I had managed to collect myself. I suppose I should just let you see." Doctor Whiley clicked again and another video sprang to life on the screen.

Luther was seated much like before, strapped to a sturdy wooden chair facing the doctor behind the camera. The skeletal face covered in bruised and cracked skin was far from the man in the last video. Even further from the man who bludgeoned men to death on the prison tape, but the eyes were keen and sharp.

"You look flustered today Doctor. I hope you're not too distracted." The voice was a rasping wheeze that grated the air.

"I'm fine thank you very much. Now let's talk about you. After all that's why we're here. I understand you've been threatening the guards? This will not be tolerated Luther."

Luther's multiple voiced laugh bubbled out from his blistered lips. "Tolerated?" There was a snideness is Luther's voice and an animal cunning in his eyes which again had that peculiar shine. "Like your poor late wife tolerated your wandering hands? Even now you can't help yourself. If only you were so persistent with helping your staff as you are in trying to bed them, your lovely little receptionist would still be alive." His lips were pulled back over yellowed teeth in a monstrous grin.

"What did you say?" there was no hiding the shock in Doctor Whiley's voice coming from off screen. Luther's reply was the voice of Jackie.

"There are these awful sounds on the other end of the line doctor. Sometimes just a whistle." He then whistled that tuneless series of notes. "Doctor Whiley, fix your head. If he can't, you'll be dead." It was unmistakably the voice of Doctor Singh. At that moment a phone rang from somewhere off-screen.

"Hello Felix Whiley, who's calling?" There followed a moment of silence. "Are you quite sure? Excuse me I'm just with a patient. Hold a moment." Footsteps headed away and a creaky door opened somewhere. "Watch him," the distant voice of Doctor Whiley said, presumably to the attending guard. "How long has she been dead?" Whiley asked in a slowly retreating voice as the door creaked closed. Luther looked directly at the camera and whistled. Doctor Whiley paused the screen.

"The call was from the police. They had gone to check on Doctor Singh as per my request and found her dead in her flat. The coroner ruled carbon monoxide poisoning. But that's not the peculiar thing. He said that she had been dead for at least four days." Doctor Whiley took off his glasses and polished them with a handkerchief from his pocket.

"So who was making the calls from her number?" asked Caleb.

"No one knows. The neighbours were questioned but no one was seen going in or out for days. Security cameras showed nothing either. But here's something else I can't explain." He clicked play on the paused screen. Luther stayed staring into the camera, for a moment both priests wondered whether the clip was rolling at all until Luther took a long breath in and closed his eyes. As soon his eyelids met the screen broke into a snowstorm of static. Occasional glimpses of half formed faces and strange animal sounds mixed into the general chaos of the black and white mess on the screen. It had already been playing for almost a minute when Mark piped up.

"What are we supposed to be seeing Felix?"

"Just give it a moment." The doctor wasn't looking at the screen. Purposefully diverting his gaze until the static broke and a scene of carnage appeared in its place. The once sterile room was now a canvas painted in blood. Its artist sat dead and strapped to the chair.

"Jesus, Mary and Joseph!" Caleb stood in horror and crossed himself several times clutching at his rosary. Mark also put a warding hand up to his face and sought the protection of oh his own crucifix.

"What on earth happened Felix?" Mark took a breath to steady himself in preparation of taking in the full bloody image.

"I was gone for no more than 15 minutes I assure you. I took the call from the police, spoke directly to the coroner then returned. The guard was outside the whole time and didn't hear a sound. We can't account for the missing time when the video turns to static either. All we know is, he somehow managed to bite through his own wrists despite the chest restraints which should have rendered that impossible. Take a closer look at the walls too. Those aren't just random blood spatters." Mark stood and walked closer to the screen.

"My word, you're right, there's writing. Caleb, come and look at this." Caleb was looking green around the gills but edged closer to Mark.

"Is that what I think it is?" he asked.

"Yes, Hebrew. And here." He pointed at another piece of viscera. "Aramaic. This here looks like Coptic." He stroked his chin and studied the scene more.

"I have several photos of the room and the writing for you to study at your own leisure. I believe there to be

33

several alphabets used. I asked Lydia to attempt some translations but I'm afraid things progressed too quickly to know whether she had any success." Doctor Whiley scratched his head and sighed. "Needless to say there was no saving Luther. The police arrived and I managed to smooth things over where they were concerned. The coroner had his body removed before sundown and the room was thoroughly cleaned after it had been properly documented. I had hoped that would be the last of it. But alas! The following day, following a night of disturbed sleep, I was told that Reece Sheridan had attacked a fellow patient and was now confined to his room. I told the attendant that I would be down shortly. Lydia had arrived that morning, insisting that she be here for me after the previous days events. She had pulled her plans forward in my time of need. Something I was immensely grateful for at the time. After a spot of tea with her, I headed off to assess Reece while she got to organising her room and research. I had just entered the corridor that Reece's room was on when a whistling came from his direction that made my blood run cold. That same tuneless whistle that had haunted my dreams since I took over Luther's treatment."

"You didn't mention you were having nightmares," interrupted Mark. Caleb remembered Mark's foul mood this morning after a bad nights sleep and wondered to himself.

"Maybe nightmares is too strong a word. Lets just say they were unsettling." He rubbed at the bridge of his nose. "As I said, Mr Sheridan was a well to do businessman with an eating disorder. Not uncommon. In fact this kind of thing makes up 95 percent of the treatments we offer here. He had never been violent before. Walking down that corridor though gave me a lead weight in the pit of my stomach after hearing that whistle. I braced myself and continued. When I opened the viewing hatch on his door, all I saw at first was a dark room. He had covered the window with his bedsheets and smashed the bulb in the light over head. All I could see were two disks of reflected light focused on me. I called to Reece through the hatch and the points of light disappeared only for his face to move into the shaft of light by the door coming from the open hatch. He had moved far too quickly and silently. Several feet in just a second. He simply grinned at me and with a single sentence filled me with horror. Doctor Whiley, fix your head. If he can't, you'll be dead."

Peaches had arrived with a trolley full of cakes, biscuits and pots of tea and coffee. "I thought you might be ready for a little refreshment." She parked up the trolley just to the side of the doorway. "Now, if you need anything else you just let me know."

"Thank you Peaches. That will be all." She gave Doctor Whiley a small nod of the head and quickly left.

"I hope she wasn't too upset by that," Caleb pointed at the screen that still displayed the blood splattered room. Doctor Whiley flushed a little in the gloom looking at the scene he'd left on screen.

"Oh well. No use crying over spilt milk. I'll have a chat with her later and make sure everything is okay. Perhaps we should take a small break though. Clear our heads before we continue." Doctor Whiley clicked the screen off and put the pointer to one side. He stretched and cracked his knuckles, "I know I could certainly use a coffee."

"Here here," agreed Mark as he slipped the notebook into this jacket pocket and headed to the trolley of refreshments. He noticed the tremor in his old friend's hands as Felix poured himself a large mug of steaming coffee. He hoped the stress wasn't too taxing on the old man and decided a topic change might ease his nerves as they took a short respite. "If I remember correctly, you were a research hoarder back in the day. If it took days to get her research here then it sounds like Lydia has followed in your footsteps in that regards" - Mark stirred several spoons of sugar into his own drink - "Felix here was obsessed with keeping notes on everything when we were younger," he turned to tell Caleb.

"You are not wrong there," Doctor Whiley admitted, "Half my library is my own research, not to mention the boxes of more research in the attic. In fact the attic is now home to most of Lydia's research and artifacts too. But it's true, the apple doesn't fall far from the tree. With her mother sadly gone so young, I raised her the best I could. My love of spiritual psychology obviously rubbed off on her. She's a research professor of anthropology with her specialist field being ancient religions and practises. Or at least she was," he murmured, looking forlornly into his mug.

"Best to be positive," said Caleb. He placed a comforting hand on the doctors shoulder, "We will do everything we can to put things right. Wont we Mark?"

"Of course. Have faith Felix." The three men sat for a few minutes enjoying the silence and refreshments. Mark looked at the clock on the wall. It was already past lunch; time was slipping away quickly. He yawned and took the notebook from his pocket. "Shall we crack on then? The sooner we're into it, the sooner we're out." Felix nodded agreement and took his place at the front of the room. Pointer in hand.

"Reece Sheridan." He clicked the button in his hand and the screen came to life displaying the picture of a handsome mid 40's man in an expensive suit. He had a disarming smile that stirred Caleb. "Like many busy executives, Reece had a problem with stress that manifested in a case of bulimia nervosa. He would gorge himself on food, often very expensive food in five star restaurants, then proceed to vomit the food back up. It's a condition we have seen many times and have a good track record with treating."

"What kind of executive was he?" asked Caleb.

"I believe he was involved with high end non-consumer electronics. Internal marketing I think" - Doctor Whiley flicked through several papers on the lectern - "Ah yes, that's right. The company was going through restructuring and the stress of uncertainty surrounding his position had caused his condition to become uncontrollable. He had been with us for close to eight weeks and showed excellent signs of recovery before the symptoms of possession manifested."

"And this is the day following Luther's death?" Mark noted.

"Correct. After my encounter with him at his room, things progressed very quickly. In a matter of days he had shown such striking similarities to Luther that I had no choice but the shut the centre down and send all patients beside Reece home. I cut the staff down to a skeleton crew, the same staff currently here. Lydia took in upon herself to put her research aside and instead help me treat Reece. I suppose for her it was professional curiosity as much as anything else. I know that she, like myself, has seen first-hand cases of what could be called possessions in other cultures around the world. If nothing else she could document it for her own research.

"She certainly sounds like the right person for the job," said Caleb.

"Indeed," Doctor Whiley nodded his agreement, "We held two or three sessions a day with Reece to try to understand how he had seemingly taken on the personality we had seen in Luther. He had stopped eating completely now and was deteriorating quickly. We tried to feed him via a nasogastric tube, but even the small amount we managed to get into him was vomited back out. We kept him hydrated via drip. After just eight days this is how he looked." Doctor Whiley clicked and an image that could have been the brother of Luther's hideously dessicated body glared back into the room. It was enough to make both priests clutch at their crosses and recoil.

"Remarkable," Mark recovered quicker than Caleb and was now studying the picture with great interest. "Felix, can you show the picture of Luther in this state?" he stood and walked towards the screen. Doctor Whiley fumbled with the computer and brought up the image of Luther.

"This one?" he asked.

"That's it. See here. Luther has three teeth missing. One

at the top here" - he pointed with his pen - "and these two at the bottom. Also this bruise here on his head. See how it has these four point near the hairline that go back across the bald head? Bring back Reece's picture would you." The image changed to Reece. "See here. At the edge of the hairline. It's the same marks. I wager the rest of the bruise was just covered by his hair. Look at the teeth also. Three missing. The same teeth that Luther was missing." Doctor Whiley was adjusting his glasses and taking a closer look.

"How on earth did I miss that?"

"More importantly, what does that mean?" asked Caleb.

"More than coincidence is all I'm willing to say right now. I assume you have recordings of the sessions with Reece for us too?" he asked Doctor Whiley, who was still marvelling at the picture on the screen. The question broke the hideous image's spell.

"Every patient is recorded when they are admitted. It's helpful for them to see the progress they have made when treatment is completed. This is Reece's admission tape." Doctor Whiley started the clip playing on the screen as Mark took his seat next to Caleb.

"Could you please state your name?" a bored mans voice asked from off screen.

"My name is Mr Reece Sheridan. But please, call me Reece." Reece looked in good humour, if a little tired.

"Thank you Reece. How old are you?"

"Older than my teeth but younger than my tongue," he laughed to himself. The change in his expression was more than enough indication that the interviewer didn't share in the humour, "I'm 28". The screen froze on Reece's awkward smile.

"Its hard to believe that this good looking guy is the same person as the creature in the picture," Caleb flushed a bit at his own evaluation of Reece as good looking. The comment made no impact on Doctor Whiley, but earned him a raised eyebrow and sideways glance from Mark. No doubt there would be words later.

"Here is a recording of the last session we had with him," Doctor Whiley started the next clip. Reece was strapped to a chair in much the same way Luther had been. Mitts had been secured to his hands with big leather straps no doubt due to the scratches all over his chest and arms. His head was bowed slightly. His ghoulish appearance made Caleb squirm in his seat.

"Reece? Reece can you hear me?" a womans voice, that must be Lydia, asked. Reece's eyes, under heavy brows, found the speaker with a quick intelligent glare. For the briefest moment they reflected the light in that animal way.

"We've told you before girly. Reece isn't here right now. Not in any way that matters at least." The sound of grinding teeth accompanied the inhuman chuckle.

"We want to speak to Mr Sheridan," Doctor Whiley's voice now. Reece's eyes flicked to the other person off-screen.

"But we're having so much fun with him," Reece said in a young girls voice, "Yes. Fun." This voice could have been a blocked drain gurgling.

"We demand to speak to Reece." Lydia's authoritative voice earned her a sharp look and snarling growl. Reece started to convulse slightly in small tremors. His face went blank for a moment as he took a deep rattling breath in and slumped in the chair. Eyes closed. "Reece?" The sharp inhalation as Reece sat up dead straight made both priests jump a little. Searching eyes in deep sockets darted around looking for something to focus on.

"Doctor!" Reece's panicked voice was his own, "Doctor please help me. I don't know what's happening."

"Its okay Mr Sheridan. You're safe. Just tell us what you remember," Doctor Whiley's tone was soothing and Reece seemed to settle a little.

"I...I don't know how to explain it. I can see what's happening I can feel everything, but I have no control. It's like I'm strapped to this chair but inside my own mind. If I try to..." he winced as if straining against a loud noise only he could hear, "If I try to take control, then I see horrific images. Terrifying faces in the dark." He was struggling to speak now, the tremor more pronounced. "I can't... I ca... I..." his head snapped to one side as if he'd just been slapped in the face. He slumped again unconscious.

"My god!" Lydia's arm and shoulder appeared in shot reaching for Reece and obscuring him before she stopped abruptly. "Let me go granddad."

"Don't be ridiculous Lydia, Sit down!" Doctor Whiley was stern. Lydia hesitated for a moment then jumped back from Reece as he whistled those three notes. She left the frame and there was that inhuman stare and grin again.

"You spoil all of our fun," Reece gave a mocking pout before breaking into a laugh of a dozen voices. The lights flickered and static broke out on the clip, "Doctor Whiley, fix your head. If he can't, you'll be dead. We know which one Luther was. Which one will Reece be?"

"What do you know about Luther?" Doctor Whiley's

voice betrayed his shock.

"Still asking all the wrong questions," Reece taunted.

"Fine then. I will ask a question," Lydia said, "Who are you?"

"Ah, a good question, but one with many answers. I will try explain in words you might understand. The dead, the never dead and the never born. They all have voices. All have stories. I am just a messenger for them. The stories must be told." Reece went into another convulsion before losing consciousness again. The clip stopped.

"That night, an alarm was sounded. Gary the security guard found Reece hanging from the light fitting. The noose had been fashioned from one of my own ties. I can't explain how he got it." Doctor Whiley rubbed his temple in exasperation, "We can't even explain how he managed to pull it off with his hands still bound in mitts."

"Now I understand why there was such limited information given to the diocese." Mark stood and put his notebook and pen into his jacket pocket again. He adjusted his glasses with a sigh, "You haven't reported Reece's death have you? Of course not. If you had you wouldn't be able to hold the police at bay. The evidence is too damning."

"You're right," Doctor Whiley sat. The exhaustion clear on his face now, "I was fully intending to call the police first thing the following morning. However, Lydia came to me in the early hours waking me and saying she had found something important in her research notes. I followed her to her room as she babbled about Syria and oracles and Babylonian stories. I was not awake enough to pay any attention. Her room was a mess of books and papers strewn about. Obviously something had struck a nerve with her and like a hound with a scent she had been up all night looking for answers. She was crouched among some books and rifling through papers when something happened to snap me out of that lingering sleep. She whistled. Those same three blood chilling notes. She carried on talking, seeming oblivious to her own act. When she finally look at me though, those eyes reflected the light. 'Are you alright?' she asked me. I feigned illness and excused myself. I had Gary and Marcy on hand to restrain her when I returned later. But they weren't needed. When we got to the room Lydia was just standing there, in the middle of the room. Grinning like a loon and waiting for us. I told her we had a special room for her to stay in temporarily and she nodded, unblinking, and followed us to a secure room, no questions asked."

"Felix. That's awful. I understand why you did what you did now." Caleb had gone over to the doctor and crouched next to his seat to comfort him.

"Where is Reece's body?" asked Mark.

"In our own morgue, in the basement."

"And how long has Lydia been in isolation?"

"Its been three days since that morning in her room."

"You work quickly Felix," Mark nodded in admiration, "It's not everyone that can get the diocese to have a case investigated in such a short time."

"Well after all we went through, and the help I've given you in the past, it seemed only fitting that I call you to return the favour." Felix raised an eyebrow at Mark. Caleb thought he saw Mark's mood darken for a moment.

"Besides, the right word in the right ear and its amazing

what can be done. Isn't that right?" Mark grunted in agreement.

"When can we see Lydia?" asked Caleb helping Doctor Whiley to his feet.

"I think it's probably best that we wait till the tomorrow now. We've covered a lot of ground today." Both Mark and Caleb nodded at each other "You'll want time to digest it all I'm sure." said Felix.

"Are you sure we shouldn't see her now?" asked Mark.

"I'm sure. She's being cared for and sedated. She's perfectly safe right now."

"Then I'd like to check Reece's body first thing," said Mark, "It'll give us a chance at least to go through some of those patient files and recordings you have ready for us."

"Of course. After we've eaten I will have everything taken to the library. I won't join you there myself, I'll let you have some space while you go through them. Besides, I could do with a good nights sleep." Doctor Whiley suddenly looked every day of his age.

"Thank you Felix," Caleb smiled warmly at the old man, "We really do appreciate it."

They cleaned themselves up for dinner in their respective rooms and found Felix waiting for them in the communal dining room with Peaches once more manning her station by the stove.

"Here they are," She greeting in her bubbly, greasy-spoon manner, "Come in, come in. Sit down otherwise you'll make the place look untidy." Felix rolled his eyes and gave a little shake of his head at Peaches, as the two men joined him. "I've made a fish pie. Thought it was a safe bet being Friday and all. I've also got chips, beans, peas, potato waffles and if you want them I can heat up some spaghetti hoops. You might well look at me like that Felix, but its better to have guests fed and food left over than send these poor men to bed hungry." She stood glaring at Doctor Whiley brandishing a ladle in one hand with and her other had thrust against her hip.

"I don't think there's any worry of that Peaches. Your food is always excellent and plentiful," he said almost apologetically.

"Well if you don't mind, I'll leave you to help yourselves. There's this amazing box-set I'm dying to finish about big cats," she told Caleb directly, "I'm going to snuggle up with my two favourite men, Ben and Jerry, and watch it." She took off her apron and headed towards the door. She called over her shoulder as she left. "There's a crumble in the oven that'll still be warm, custard in the big copper pot and ice cream in the freezer. Don't open the pineapple chunks and try not to make a mess." She turned to give Doctor Whiley a raised eyebrow at the mention of pineapple chinks. " See you in the morning boys." She left.

They ate heartily and chatted easily, the reason for their visit and the circumstances surrounding it forgotten for this short time. Doctor Whiley had opened a bottle of wine for them to enjoy, which they drank from mugs emblazoned with pharmaceutical logos. After the fish pie, which was very good, if a little burnt, Caleb served them all crumble which he was happy to discover was apple. He slathered each gooey slab of dessert in a thick vanilla custard; aromatic steam flowing as he balanced the three bowls over to the table.

"I'm so happy to see you looking so well Mark. I thought for sure after all that messy business you'd retire." Doctor Whiley looked questioningly at his old friend as he shovelled a large spoonful of crumble into his mouth. Mark looked none too happy as he swallowed his own mouthful.

"What messy business is that?" asked Caleb.

"It was nothing. Just a misunderstanding in my former parish." Mark looked down at his dessert signalling the matter closed.

"I'm sorry old boy, I spoke out of turn. I just assumed you would have told your student everything. But you're right, it was just a misunderstanding." Doctor Whiley feigned chagrin for Caleb who just gave a little shrug, "So tell me young man, do you have a parish of your own?"

"Me?" Caleb snorted at the question, "No no. I'm waiting for a suitable placement, but in the meantime I float around. Kind of like a substitute teacher for churches. Every now and then I get called to join Mark on one of these investigations. Its interesting work."

"I'm sure it is," nodded Doctor Whiley, "I know when I used to come along as a medical adviser there were some amazing cases. Mark, what was the name of that red headed girl? You know, the one who drew stigmata on herself."

"Lucy Brannigan," Mark smiled, "Wow, I haven't thought about her for years. She had a thing for priests," He told Caleb, turning to face him. "She'd recently seen some movie and thought if she had stigmata she could get an exorcism and the priest would fall in love with her." He clasped his hands by his chin for a moment and fluttered his eyes in a mock virginal pose. "Of course the problem was she was scared of blood, would faint at the sight of it. So she had the genius idea to use her mums lipstick to draw wounds on her hands and feet," Mark laughed.

"Do you remember that old battle axe mother of hers?" Doctor Whiley joined in the laughter, then poorly imitated the mother. "That was my best Rimmel you little cow!" All three men laughed. They chatted for a little while longer, reminiscing about some of the more absurd cases. The haunted house that was caused by a cat getting into the drywall. The voices in the attic from an old baby monitor picking up a taxi firm. The possessed doll that was just a home to dormice. Left over custard had congealed on the sides of bowls by the time Doctor Whiley finally called it a night and left Mark and Caleb to browse the files in the library.

"I expected there to be more boxes," said Caleb as he lifted the lid of one of the three cardboard office cartons. Mark was helping himself to a can of coke from the globe bar.

"Want one?" He held the can up for Caleb to see. Caleb nodded and deftly caught the can that Mark threw to him. "Well we had better get cracking. You take the right box, I'll take the left one and we can split the one in the middle." They each carried a box over to the fireplace and sat in the warm glow of the gas fire that had been lit ready for them. The files inside, sparse as they were, covered nearly all the information Doctor Whiley had given them that afternoon. There were more pictures here though. And cassettes which were named and dated. "Did you bring your tape player with you?" Mark looked up from a particularly gruesome photo of Luther to see Caleb studying a similar photo of Reece.

"Yes its in my bag in my room," he said absently without looking up, "These scratches on Reece, I think they're letters." He pointed them out to Mark as he passed over the photo.

"I believe you're right." Mark said studying the bloodied grooves that were being shown to him. Why don't you work on the tapes and I'll take the pictures. Might as well split our efforts properly."

"Good idea," Caleb said through a yawn, "Excuse me. Just a bit tired."

"It's fine. Take the tapes to your room and make a start on them when you're ready. I'll stay here a little longer and see if I can make head or tail of this writing. We'll both be better for a good night's sleep I have no doubt."

"OK, I'll see you in the morning then." Caleb collected the dozen or so tapes from the boxes and left Mark alone in the library. Once he had gone, Mark got to work. He rested his notebook on the arm of the chair so he could scribble in it as he tried to decipher the words rendered in flesh and blood. Several times he shuddered and looked around the room. The feeling of eyes studying him, as he in turn studied the photos, made him uncomfortable. Then the moment would pass and be forgotten. As he was stuck into a particularly juicy transcription of a piece of biblical text in one of Luther's photos, he suddenly had the sensation of someone standing right behind him. Like a shadow had crept up in silence and was about to strike out at him. He jumped up from his seat, turning as he did to confront this intruder into his private bubble. There was nothing but empty space behind him. No shadow, no person. He mopped a bead of sweat from his brow with a shaky hand and decided to call it a night. He was shocked to see it was 3am when he looked at his watch. Cursing himself for staying up too late, he gathered up the photos into a single box and took it to his room, shutting off the fire on his way.

Morning came too soon for both men. Caleb had already finished eating by the time Mark joined him in the kitchen diner. Caleb looked how Mark felt, which he supposed left himself looking much worse. He was right.

"My dear you do look a fright," Peaches said, "I'm sorry, I don't mean to offend. Are you feeling alright?"

"I'm fine thank you. Just a little tired." Mark sat across from Caleb and rubbed his temples trying to stimulate his brain to catch up with his body.

"I told you those mattresses are no good. If you ask me, you'll do better to sleep on the floor. I've set out some cereal for this morning. I hope that's alright. I have to nip into town so I'm a bit rushed off my feet. Coffee here too."

"Thank you Peaches. Do you have any aspirin?" Mark had no luck waking his brain up and there was a buzzing behind his eyes as a migraine threatened to manifest.

"I don't but I'm sure Felix can help you with that when you see him. Now I must be off. Help yourself to whatever you need." Peaches took the tea towel off of her shoulder and gave the counter a quick wipe down as she made her way out, hanging the small rag on a hook as she left.

"She's not wrong you know," Caleb said as Mark

poured himself a bowl of mini, frosted shredded wheat and drowned them in cold milk. "You do look a fright. What time did you get to bed last night? It was gone midnight when I got to my room. I didn't realise we'd been at it so long."

"A little after three," Mark sighed, "But even when I got to sleep it wasn't restful. I was tossing and turning all night. Had a couple of weird dreams too."

"Me too. Not the tossing and turning, but the dreams. I stayed up for another hour or so when I got back to my room and listened to some of the tapes. Oh I've made some transcripts by the way. Pretty standard possession theatrics by all counts. Cursing and threatening and speaking in tongues. But, I don't know. There was something about the voices; they unnerved me more than I expected. When I went to sleep it felt like they followed my into my dreams. I don't remember anything specific but I woke up before six this morning with them still ringing in my head." Caleb looked worried.

"Why don't you take some time this morning to pray for guidance. I can make a start on Reece's body by myself. Maybe you can take a nap too." He placed a comforting hand on Caleb's forearm and decided not to comment on the slight moisture rimming Caleb's eyes. Just over-tiredness making him emotional, he thought. Mark ate his cereal and they both finished their coffees in silence before making their way back to their rooms. Caleb took the advice given to him and, after showering and praying for strength and peace of mind, he settled in for a nap. Mark, however, took his shower, and after collecting his things set out to look for the basement morgue.

Twenty minutes of searching and coming up against locked door after locked door had him lost. The buzzing behind his eyes growing with his frustration. He was just about to retrace his step back when a gruff female voice came echoing along to him.

"Lost Father?" asked Marcy.

"That obvious huh?" he said, rather embarrassed.

"Looking for?" she grunted back.

"The morgue. You couldn't show me the way I suppose?" She grunted an affirmation at him and started walking back the way she had come. Mark all but jogged to catch her up. They walked in silence for several minutes along corridors and down a flight of stairs before reaching the familiar entrance hall of the hospital. The ficus still hadn't been watered, Mark noted; its fronds starting to crisp and brown at the tips. The passed through quickly with Marcy keeping an even marching pace. They headed down the corridor where Gary had taken their bags for inspection and after a couple more security gates she stopped at the top of a flight of stairs.

"Down there. Second door." She turned on her heels to leave him, no doubt going back to whatever job she'd been intending to do before finding the lost priest.

"Thank you. If either yourself or Gary see Father Kedge, would you let him know I'll be fine on my own. No use him getting lost as well." She didn't break her stride as Mark spoke to her. Just turned her head to see him from the corner of her eye and nodded. The stairway descended into semi darkness. Mark flicked the light switch but nothing happened. He flicked it back and forth a few times, but still nothing. Nor were there any other switches.

"Oh well," he said to the darkness and took a deep breath in. Slowly he started down the stairs. There was just enough light to see by but it still made him feel uncomfortable. He could see the second door along since there was light spilling out under the closed door into the darkness. "Hello?" he called out. No answer came. The threat of the migraine returned again. He grasped the door handle and pushed the door inward with a creak. "Hello?" he said again poking his head into the cool neon light of the refrigerated room. Happy to discover no one living in the room, he entered fully and closed the door behind him. The tiled floor and walls made every sound echo as he walked to the table in the centre of the room. Evidently someone had been here to set up the room for him since there was already a body covered with a white sheet on the examination table. The tag around the toe along with the folder on a small stainless steel trolley both read 'Reece Sheridan'. The chill in the room was coming from the bank of nine body storage drawers, arranged in a square and set into the wall near the foot of Reece's body. The middle one, no doubt where Reece had been stored till recently, had been left ajar. Mark pushed it closed and blew warm air into his hands to keep the chill at bay. He flicked through the folder, bracing himself, before having to uncover what remained of Reece. The papers inside gave minimal information. He took his own notebook and pen out and put them with the folder on the trolley. Moving to the top of the table he grasped the edges of the sheet and pulled it down to reveal the head and shoulders of Reece. His face was frozen in a contorted expression. Mark had seen many bodies before but this one created a lead weight in the pit of his stomach. He swallowed against the sour taste in his mouth and uncovered the rest of the body, leaving the sheet in a crumpled pile at the corpse's feet. A box of mauve nitrile gloves had been left on the shelf of the trolley, below the folder. He double gloved each hand then set about his closer examination of the body. Mark had seen only glimpses of Reece's arms and neck in the photos he had looked at. There were numerous words, in various scripts that made no sense, captured in the small shots. Reece's naked body was a ledger by comparison. The photos had not done justice to the interwoven combination of marks that covered his skin. Mark started tracing where one piece ended and another started, being drawn deeper and deeper into the web. There were declarations of love, confessions, religious texts, all in different dialects and languages. Intermingled were symbols and text which defied Mark's attempts to decipher. Similar marks he had also seen in the photos of Luther's blood splattered room. He meticulously copied everything he could. Drawn in as he was, his back soon started to ache and he found a stool in the corner of the room to use. The body was eye level when he sat and he saw that the text continued to the back of body. There was no use putting it off. He would have to flip the corpse. It took some effort and a lot of grunting but Mark slid Reece to one side of the table then rolled the body onto its front with a meaty thud. One of Reece's arms slid from the table and hung there limply from the shoulder. Mark walked around the table to place the arm back on the table top. He gripped the hand and the hand gripped back. He jumped back in fright. "Motherfucker!"

Mark was not in the habit of swearing and covered his own mouth at the unexpected outburst. He told himself that bodies twitch, it's just what happens. Rationalising the situation to alleviate his own mounting fear, something then occurred to him. He approached the body again and held the hand in his own. "Fingernail biter huh? So why the mitts? How did you scratch this all onto yourself?" he asked the dead man. He put Reece's arm back in position and continued taking notes and replicating the marks covering the poor dead man's body. Time passed in silence, only the scratch of pen on paper could be heard in room above the hum of the refrigeration unit. Mark was inspecting a particularly long piece of text on Reece's right buttock that looked to be Russian. He started to notice a chill creeping over his right hand side. He turned to the right and the body drawers. Three of the doors stood ajar, including the one that had housed Reece. He was sure he had closed it. He certainly didn't hear any noise from the heavy latches each door was fitted with. He closed them. Testing them to make sure they were closed then got back to the body. No sooner had he sat down than a metallic sound came from the area he'd just been. He looked over to see five of the doors now stood ajar. Cool air rolled from the void behind each door. It was now cold enough in the room for him to see his breath before him in a mist. Cautiously, he stood and went to the doors. Closing each one and testing them. The sensation of being watched had also returned. Just as it had been there last night. He turned to confront the shadow he felt behind him only to face empty air. The metallic sound came again and he spun on his heels to be faced with all nine doors fully open.

"Mark," the voice sent a bolt of fear through him so palpable he clutched his chest and saw white for a moment as he spun again.

"Jesus-fucking-Christ!"

In the doorway stood Caleb and Gary, "Well I ain't never heard a priest talk like that." Gary was grinning from ear to ear.

"Oh bless me Father. Forgive me." Mark was still clutching his chest and crossing his body with the other hand as he steadied himself and sat back in the stool by the body.

"Mark what happened. Are you okay?" Caleb went to his mentor and crouched in front of him, hands on his friends knees.

"I'm fine." Mark breathed heavily as he regained his composure, "Just some trouble with the body locker doors." He pointed with a thumb over too them as he closed his eyes to clear his head.

"What kind of trouble?" asked Gary walking over to them.

"They keep opening," Mark told him.

"Look fine to me," Gary answered with his hands on his hips standing in front of nine closed doors. Mark's stunned look concerned Caleb. Something had really rattled his friend.

"I'm sure it's just lack of sleep Mark. Maybe you dozed off for a second and dreamt something?" Caleb offered the flimsy excuse to both save Mark's pride and as a reason to discuss it later. Outside of this room. While he would never say it out loud, he hated the feel of the morgue. The cold sterility, he felt, robbed death of its spiritual function. Give him an open casket in a chapel any day.

"Maybe you're right," Mark said without conviction, "What are you doing here? I told Marcy to tell you I'd be fine by myself."

"She did," Gary piped up. "But when you didn't turn up for lunch Caleb and Felix thought you might have lost track of time." Mark looked at his watch. 2:30pm. As if to confirm the time his stomach growled hungrily.

"Looks like I did," Mark collected his notebook and stuffed it along with his pen into his jacket pocket. Gary was already covering Reece's body with the sheet.

"I'll come back later and put Mr Sheridan back to bed." He pointed at the corpse lockers. "Peaches has saved you some sandwiches and cakes. Follow me." Gary waltzed out of the room with a hand over his head as if he were some guide on a walking tour. Mark followed with Caleb close behind. Something seemed different to Mark. It was only when they reached the bottom of the stairs that he realised. The lights were on. He turned and stared suspiciously at the neon tubes overhead.

"You okay?" asked Caleb in a whisper and breaking Mark's focus on the now illuminated hall.

"Hm?" He looked at the younger man, "Oh yes, fine. Sorry. It's nothing." He gave Caleb a smile and they left the basement following Gary all the way back to their rooms.

After eating a light lunch and drinking a very large sweet coffee in his room, Mark felt better about this mornings trip to the morgue. Maybe Caleb was right.

Neither of them had been sleeping well, although he hoped that his young charge hadn't been plagued by the nightmares he had since arriving. Young girls covered in blood and muck, dancing in circles and singing horrendous rhymes which escaped his waking thoughts. He had even tried to write down what he recollected as soon as he woke in a cold sweat, but all he could recall was eyes shining in the gloom as they starred at him. Someone knocked on his door.

"Mark? I think we're ready to go down to the maximum wing now." It was Doctor Whiley. He had met them on their return from the morgue and with a look of concern at Mark's tired state. He had told him to rest for a while in his room and Peaches would bring his lunch to him. An hour had now passed and Mark felt much more himself.

"The door is unlocked. Come in," Mark called out. The door swung open and there stood Doctor Whiley, Marcy and Caleb.

"You look better," noted Caleb.

"Indeed. Peaches' sandwiches and coffee are a tonic to the body and mind," Felix winked, "Shall we make our way? I have the room all set up and the, um, patient is restrained and ready."

"After you," Mark gestured, picking up his bag to leave and admiring the detachment of his old friend. Despite his demeanour, though, both Mark and Caleb could see the apprehension on Doctor Whiley's face. It almost came off of him in waves which became stronger as they followed him, their footsteps echoing through the corridors. After Marcy let them through several security gates, they turned the corner into a corridor much like all the others. One of the overhead lights buzzed as it occasionally flickered on and off. Doctor Whiley fumbled through a mass of keys on a ring before holding two of them up to the priests.

"Here they are," he said triumphantly. He walked over to two doors which stood side by side. "This is the observation room," he told them, "I will be in here; there is a one way mirror which allows me to view this treatment room." He put a hand on the other door. "If you need anything at all then Marcy will be outside the door. Just call." They all looked at the she-hulk who nodded and took a position beside the treatment room door, standing to attention like a sentry on duty.

"Well then," Mark took a deep breath and readied himself. "Lets begin."

Maybe it was the thought of Luther and Reece and the horrors they had both become, but whatever the two priests expected to greet them in the well lit and sterile examination room, it was not this mid 20's, well-groomed girl in jeans, boots and a loose cardigan. She had a look of utter boredom on her face.

"You have got to be kidding me. Really grandpa, Priests?" she glared at the mirror and tutted loudly whilst rolling her eyes. She turned her attention back to the two men who had entered the room, "Forgive me for not standing, I'm a bit tied up as you can see." Caleb and Mark looked at each other in confusion as Lydia Crossed one leg over the other. Her legs were the only part of her besides her head not strapped to the chair she was sitting in. Thick tanned leather straps held her around the chest, waist and forearms. Raising an eyebrow at his companion, Mark indicated for Caleb to follow and left the room.

Marcy held her position as Mark knocked on the door of Whiley's observation room. The door opened.

"Is this some kind of joke Felix? She looks completely normal to me" Mark's hushed tone barely contained his frustration.

"I swear to you Mark. This is just an act. I've seen her do things. Say things. We all have." He indicated to Marcy who still stayed unmoved. Mark huffed and pinched the bridge of his nose.

"Isn't this exactly why we're here Mark? The greatest trick the devil ever played was to convince mankind he doesn't exist after all." Caleb's optimism did little to change Mark's mood, but he had a point. They were here to investigate and that is exactly what he would do.

"Fine," agreed Mark. "We'll need to perform some of the standard tests. I have to be honest though Felix, she seems fine."

"Please just trust me. Have some faith," pleaded Doctor Whiley.

"Faith is no problem for me, I'm just having a hard time believing." Mark turned and entered back into the examination room with Caleb close on his heels.

"Did you forget a bible or something?" Lydia pursed her lips at the return of the priests.

"I don't think there is any call for sarcasm Lydia," Mark said taking a seat in one of the two chairs that had been set up facing Lydia, "You know as well as we do that your grandfather only asked us here to help."

"He just wants to make sure you're okay Lydia," said Caleb taking the other seat.

"Well it seems you both have me at a disadvantage," she

looked at them both disapprovingly.

"Forgive us. I am Father Eskil, and my companion here is Father Kedge." He indicated to Caleb who was rummaging in his bag and placing a variety of items on a small table by the side of them. Mark simply unsnapped the clasp of his bag which he had placed on the floor beside him and reached in, pulling out a black leather bound bible.

"How very formal. In that case you can call me Ms Whiley," she raised her eyebrow, "Are you going to tell me a bedtime story father Eskil?" she nodded to the Bible.

"You understand why we are here," he said to her as a matter of fact, dismissing her comment about the bible, "Let's all just relax and get through this. The sooner we're done the sooner you'll be free to go."

"Why don't you tell us how you ended up here?" suggested Caleb. Lydia sighed heavily.

"If it'll get me out of here then fine. I was at my office in Oxford writing up research notes from my latest expedition. After eight months on a hot dig site in the middle east then another six months camping in the black forest transcribing pictograms, I was glad to be home. If I'd know then that this is where I'd end up, I would have stayed in Jordan." She turned to face the mirror and glared disapprovingly. "No offence Grandpa but your hospitality stinks." Caleb stifled a grin and looked down at his bag, trying hard not to laugh. She was funny.

"Jordan. The Black Forest. It sounds like you travel a lot for your work. What exactly are you researching?" asked Mark.

"No offence," She cocked her head to patronise the

older man, "I just don't think someone so devout to a belief system as young as Christianity would be interested in the ethnographic origins of ancient global religious practises. I'm also not in the most comfortable position to be able to explain it fully." She pulled on the wrist restraints to make her point. "Look, I'm sorry." She sighed and softened. "I just want to get out of here. Look, I'll be level with you. My financial backers for the last expedition weren't happy that the research didn't bring anything new to light. Or at least anything that they could sell for a profit. So I sold my offices in Oxford to pay them back and came here to have a fresh start."

"Oh that sounds awful. It not easy starting a new chapter," Caleb's consoling tone calmed the atmosphere that had been building in the room and Lydia gave him a smile, tears brimming in her eyes. Mark noted then that Lydia was missing three teeth and his interest was piqued. Now that he looked closer at her, was that a bruise on her head just peeping out under the hairline? A small lead weight was forming in his stomach. He took out his notebook and wrote 'Teeth' intending to show Caleb and alert his attention to the fact when out of nowhere Lydia said.

"Careful Caleb." At that moment Caleb's Bible fell from his lap on to the floor and he reached forward to pick it up. As he lent over with a confused look, his face suddenly impacted with Lydia's right boot as she kicked him hard enough to send him sprawling back clutching his bleeding nose. Mark jumped up to help his young friend.

"Fuck, Fuck! I think she's broken my fucking nose!"

Caleb howled through a bloody handkerchief that Mark had wadded against his friends face. Behind him, Mark could hear a quiet chuckle, as if several children were giggling all at once. He turned to see Lydia sitting there. The leg ending in a bloodied boot neatly crossed over the other leg, and while the sound of giggling continued, she just smiled at him. Her eyes flashed a silver reflection as Mark stood and allowed Marcy, who had entered quickly on hearing the disturbance, escort Caleb out of the room. Mark followed, bags in hand. As the door closed behind them he heard a tuneless whistle. Doctor Whiley was closing the door of his own room as he joined them in the hall. He took Caleb's face in his hands and checked his eyes.

"Pupils looks good. How many fingers am I holding up?" He took a step back and held up three fingers.

"Three," moaned Caleb through a handful off cotton handkerchief that was more red than white, "It's broken isn't it."

"Quite possibly. Lets get you down to an examination room and I can take a proper look. Mark?" Doctor Whiley motioned towards Caleb and Mark took him by the arm and out of Marcy's meaty clutches. Once they got him to the room a quick examination confirmed that Caleb's nose was indeed broken. "I'm going to have to reset it before I secure it in place. I'm not going to lie, this is going to hurt." He raised the head of the bed and filled a tray with medical equipment and bandages. "Now just lay back and close your eyes." Caleb was trembling as he laid back, he hadn't let go of Mark's hand the whole time. Doctor Whiley put on a pair of gloves, each snapping sound making Caleb jump just a little. "Okay Caleb, you're in good hands. Now I'm going to put my hands on your nose and count to three. When I get to three I'll reset the nose and we can secure it in place." Caleb whimpered agreement.

"You can do this. Come on now." Mark was encouraging the poor young priest. Doctor Whiley readied himself and held Caleb's nose with a gentle touch.

"One." He winked at Mark as he make a quick jerking movement with his hands and shouted "Two!" The sound of the cartilage crunching and the nose popping back into place along with Caleb's agonised cry all but drown out any other noise. It had been too much for Caleb. He passed out.

He awoke later in his room, tucked into bed in a clean pair of pyjamas. Mark was sat beside him reading through a file Caleb couldn't make out. His head felt groggy as he tried to sit up.

"Hey hey! Lay down." Mark paced a gentle hand on Caleb's chest and pushed him back into the sheets, "You need to rest."

"What happened?" Caleb's voice was raspy from the dried blood that had coated the back of his throat. He touched a hand to his face and felt the hard bandage that had been secured there, "Is it fixed?"

"You passed out is all. I'm not surprised. We got you fixed up though and carried you back here."

"Marcy?" he said closing his eyes.

"Marcy. I swear that woman is like a shire horse," Mark chuckled as he smoothed a piece of hair back behind his friends ear. He knew how Caleb felt about him. Caleb had a lousy poker face for that sort of thing; too innocent. Mark may not have reciprocated the feelings, but he did care for the boy. "I've put some water on the bedside table. Try to get some rest. You'll have a headache in the morning and a black eye or two I shouldn't wonder." Caleb groaned an acknowledgement as he slipped to sleep. Hopefully the drugs Doctor Whiley had given him would help him sleep right through to the morning. Mark left him to sleep and went to find Felix. He was in the library pouring two large glasses of amber relief.

"I'm so sorry Mark. She hasn't been violent like that at all. I had no way to know. How is he?" Doctor Whiley took the drinks to the fireplace where Mark had already slumped in to one of the armchairs covering his eyes with a hand.

"He'll be fine," he said with a huge sigh of relief. Uncovering his eyes, he took a glass of brandy and took a large gulp.

"Are you okay old boy?" Doctor Whiley lit one of his slender cigars and slipped the thin gold case back into his jacket pocket.

"Honestly, I'm a bit more shaken up than usual. I thought what had happened today had just put me on edge, but..." He shook his head and took another large gulp of brandy, "Felix she looks so much like Mary." The sound of his daughter's name made Doctor Whiley pause for a moment. "I'm sorry Felix, I know you don't like to talk about her. It just caught me off guard is all." An unexpected tear clouded his sight.

"That's all a long time in the past old boy. I know she

came to you for spiritual guidance. I was hardly in a state to deal with her myself after her mother's death. Its no wonder she kept the pregnancy from me. A14 year old unmarried new mother who was still grieving the death of her own mother; the suicide was inevitable. I've made my peace with it, and you should to." He took a long drag on his cigar and exhaled the smoke through his nose.

"I thought I had. Losing touch with you all those years ago somehow made it easier to bury the memory. That sounds awful to say, I'm sorry. It just feels like I'm here for a reason, to fix the past or something."

"You don't really believe that do you?"

"Honestly?" Mark sat back in the seat and drained the last of his drink, "I don't know what I believe these days." They sat in silence watching the flickering fire and drinking.

"Morning sunshine." Mark was still in a dressing gown and unshaven as he stood in the doorway of Caleb's room with a tray in hand, "Peaches sends her best wishes. I told her Felix ordered you not be disturbed. I thought your head and ears would thank me." Caleb rubbed the sleep from his eyes and immediately regretted knocking the bridge of his nose with a finger.

"Ouch!. Son of a-"

"Careful," warned Mark, "We had enough language yesterday." He smiled but Caleb could see how weary Mark looked this morning. The grey in his hair and stubble seemed more pronounced somehow. Dark circles were starting to form under his eyes. That sparked something in his brain.

"Do I have a black eyes?" he touched gingerly at the edges of his face near his eyes.

"You're lucky," he answered, placing the tray over Caleb's lap. Its thin, metal, fold-down legs made a decent enough bed table. "Only the one black eye, and its not too bad. Want to see?" Caleb nodded as he tucked into a slice of well buttered toast. He felt famished. Mark brought over a hand mirror and held it in front of Caleb for him to peer into. It wasn't as bad as he'd imagined after all. He felt like a huge bandage was strapped to his face and but in reality a hard flesh coloured film had been placed over his padded nose. Aside from a small piece of metal protruding from it at the bridge of the nose and his right eye which had blackened a little, it didn't look too bad. He immediately felt more at ease. That is until he took a sip of tea and breathing out through his nose heard a distinct whistle come from it.

"Was that me?" the look of shock on his face was too much for Mark who broke into laughter.

"I'm sorry" he said taking a seat on the bed at Caleb's feet. "Its just a relief. The whistle is probably just swelling. We can ask Felix to check it out later." Mark stretched and yawned, deftly swiping a piece of toast for himself from the tray across Caleb's lap. "I'll leave you to it then. Oh, whilst I remember, Felix said not to get your nose wet, you know, because of the dressing. Maybe just have a wash with a flannel today. Don't worry about a shower. I'll come back for you when we're ready to set off. I want to have a chat with Felix before then if I can." He took a large bite of toast and left Caleb to it. Caleb sat there and examined his face in the mirror some more while he demolished the breakfast. Standing up to get ready, he felt light-headed and sat back down again. A few deep breaths and a promise to himself to take it easier and he was soon getting washed and dressed for the day. He sat and held a bible in his hand, spine down, and let it open to a random page to read from. A silly little habit of his but he often found comfort in the random passages that came to him. Today was Daniel 2:22 'He reveals deep and hidden things; he know what lies in darkness, and light dwells with him.' He decided to pray for a moment and contemplate the words, but instead of peace he had a growing unease in the pit of his stomach. The more he acknowledged it, the more it grew. He had the sensation of the room around him dragging him down. Deeper and deeper in a twisting stretching motion that made him nauseous.

"I've had a quick chat with Felix, he's going to.... my goodness are you okay?" Mark had dressed and was going to lay out the days plans to his friend. But entering the room he found Caleb sat with a bible clutched in a white knuckled hand. His face had a pale green hue as sweat beaded across his forehead. He rushed over and released the book from his grip. Caleb took a deep cleansing breath and opened his eyes as Mark patted his forehead with a towel, "What happened?"

"I'm fine," Caleb said, fighting back the urge to vomit, "Probably just some residual effect of whatever painkillers I was given. I have to say though, I'm not looking forward to going back in to an examination room with Lydia."

"Well that's what I was going to tell you. I think its safer for all concerned if we aren't so confined when we see her.

We don't want a repeat of yesterday. I spoke to Felix and he agreed. The patient common room is not being used at the moment, on account of there being no patients. He's going to make arrangements for us to continue there. In the meantime, we can spend this morning looking through her things in her room. It'll give you the chance to take things easy, which by the looks of it, you need."

"I have a request of my own though," said Caleb.

"Oh yes? What's that then?"

"Tea and biscuits. And plenty of both," he said with a cheeky grin, looking much more like his normal self. Mark laughed and pulled Caleb to his feet.

"I'm sure I can have that arranged for you."

By late morning, Caleb was on his fourth cup of tea and had made his way through two thirds of a packet of chocolate fingers. He sat contentedly on the floor of Lydia's room among scattered papers, pieces of pottery and other decorative items of unknown origin. Mark paced as he read a similar file to the one Caleb had open on his lap. He'd found the current file under a worn cricket ball and was tossing the ball in the air and catching it as he paced. The rhythm had become hypnotic to Caleb, who had stopped really reading and was simply staring at the pictures in his file. He looked up when the expected thud of ball in palm didn't come.

"I don't know if any of this is helping," Mark sighed, "I'd have more luck deciphering Reece's body in the morgue than making sense of these notes. She's as bad as Felix with these files. Just take a look at these maps." He pointed to several maps that had been pinned to the wall with yet more notes pinned on top in various places,

"Fairy tales, legends, superstitions. Are these really something for an academic to study? Look at this guy." He held up a picture of what appeared to be a shaman, dressed head to toe in a feathered cloak with a reptilian mask on. He read out the scribbled note on the back, "'Congo, Shaman Dhipta, conduit of Ashnata. Makes a lovely beetle brew.' I mean really!" he said dismissively as he tucked the photo back in the file and slapped the whole thing down on the table. "There's just no rhyme or reason to any of this. I found a whole box over there of old police reports next to newspaper clippings of mermaid sightings. How are we supposed to argue that a person is or isn't possessed when they are-" he gestured around him at the mess in the room "a conspiracy theorist?"

"You have to admit though. There's is some really interesting stuff here. Let's just hope we aren't dealing with this little guy." He flashed a mischievous grin as he held up a picture for Mark to see. It was a wood carving of a little downtrodden looking imp-like creature, below was written the word 'Yattering'. "I don't think being in this room is helping though. I can only read so much about divination and vassal virgins in one morning." He held up another picture of women in Greek garb dancing in the mouth of a cave. "Lets see if Felix is ready for us. They should be set up by now surely." Mark agreed. They left Lydia's room as they found it, a disorganised mess. The decision to stop off at their rooms turned out to be a fortuitous one as Doctor Whiley was there waiting for them.

"Gentlemen. Caleb, how are you feeling today?" Doctor Whiley started poking Caleb's face without invitation and examining the cast and bruising around Caleb's eye. He tutted several times out loud. "Well that's certainly going to be a shiner." He mock punched Caleb on the shoulder, "But you'll live. It could have been a lot worse believe me."

"Uh, thanks Felix," Caleb said pulling away a little, "I'm actually not too bad now the meds have worn off. A bit sore, you know. But otherwise fine."

"Excellent. We've just about set things up for you. I'm afraid there's nowhere outside the room for me to observe from." He scratched his head. "I know I'm not supposed to be involved Mark, but would you mind me sitting in? I promise not to say or do anything. I just don't want to miss anything and it will save you having to debrief me later." Mark considered for a moment. Their shared history had given him pause to begin with, but it was history after all.

"Very well. But remember Felix, it's the churches wishes that you not get involved. Nothing personal you understand."

"Of course, of course. I will be as quiet as a mouse or quieter." He mimed locking his mouth closed and putting the key in his jacket pocket. A warm smile relaxing his face, "What is the plan?" He looked back and forth between the two priests.

"Well usually we would pray over a person to incite a reaction of some kind. But we've already got that I would say" Caleb pointed to his nose. The whistling nose as he breathed out punctuated his point. Doctor Whiley could plainly see how yesterday's events had shifted Caleb's thoughts towards a confirmed possession. Mark was not to easy to gauge.

"We've decided to move to a more traditional methodology. I'm hoping that prayers of dedication and sanctification in the presence of holy icons will bring forth whatever plagues Lydia, be that demon or disease of the mind." He gave Doctor Whiley a raised eyebrow, "You understand what I'm saying?"

"Of course," nodded Felix, "Just like the Prentice boy." Mark's eyes widened and he seemed to choke for a second at whatever memory came to him.

"Yes. Just like that. Hopefully with a better outcome," He eyed his old friend for a moment before Caleb interrupted.

"Felix. I have to ask this. Did Lydia know we were coming?"

"Not that I'm aware of. Although under the circumstances it was inevitable I would call for the church's aid. We'd discussed it as an option for Reece. Why do you ask dear boy?"

"Its just that. Well before she did this, she called me Caleb. I mean I think she did. Didn't she? My heads still a bit fuzzy about it all." He put his hand to his head and shrunk back a little as his cheeks reddened a shade.

"You're right," Mark said thoughtfully, "She did use your first name. I'm almost positive we didn't tell her those. Just as you asked Felix. You didn't say anything to her? Not even accidentally mentioning our names?"

"Absolutely not! You know I have more sense than that. I may be old but I'm still a stickler for the scientific method. I wouldn't want to interfere like that."

"Of course. I'm sorry." Mark quickly took out his

notebook, jotted something down and put the book back intro his jacket pocket, "Just have to make sure. You understand."

"Well its no use us standing around speculating," said Caleb looking at his watch, "We should get started." Within just a few moments, both men were following Doctor Whiley through more abandoned sterile corridors. They each carried their leather bags containing all the items they would need for the prayers. Even unlit, the odour of the altar incense could be smelled as they walked along. Wafting up from the mess of crosses, candles and other items in Mark's bag that might be needed. Caleb was surprised to see Gary waiting for them outside the room. After yesterday's attack from Lydia, he had assumed Marcy would be a better candidate to police the room. Gary had a warm and disarming smile, though, which seemed to alleviate any brief misgivings Caleb had.

"Morning fellas. I've had a ciggie and I'm good to go," he appeared in good spirits, "Oh looks like Marcy wasn't kidding about your nose. Fingers crossed she don't break anything else today, you know what I mean?" he chuckled to himself.

"We'll be extra careful," said Caleb as he walked past Gary, following Doctor Whiley and Mark who were opening the door to the common room. He clapped Gary on the shoulder as he passed in friendly camaraderie at what they were about to enter into. He assumed the medication must still be playing with his senses a little as Gary's flesh seemed to shift slightly under his hand. Like wet sand in a bag.

"After you," Doctor Whiley was saying as he stepped

aside from the open door. Mark entered, followed by Caleb who was shaking the cobwebs from his brain. The room was cool and still. Caleb could see his breath is small puffs in front of him as he entered. Mark had been obscuring his view but now he'd gone off to the side to start taking things out of his bag, Caleb had a clear view of Lydia. She was strapped much as she had been the previous day to a sturdy wooden chair. Caleb was glad to note that her feet had also been secured this time. He had to avert his gaze though as she stared back at him with such unflinching malice that it had him wanting to leave. He looked over at Mark instead and locked eyes with him. No words were needed for Caleb to understand that Mark felt the same as he did. Lydia's eyes followed Caleb as he helped Mark set up. As they both took out candles and oils and laid them besides their bibles Mark looked up a few times at Lydia. If it wasn't for the small puffs of vapour leaving her mouth, he would be hard pressed to know if she was breathing. She just stared at them both. Occasionally her eyes caught the light and reflected that silvery gleam at them. Caleb placed a small pinch of pungent resin onto the brass censer and lit the charcoal briquette, sending small tendrils of acrid flowery smoke into the air.

"I think we're ready Father," Caleb said as he draped a stole around his neck, the long ends dusting the floor as be bent to pick up his own bible. A small click and whir made them both turn and see Doctor Whiley taking a seat in the corner by the door. He had clicked a Dictaphone on and for a second was murmuring something into it under his breath. He then pointed the microphone of the small device into the room and nodded that he was ready. Gary also took a deep breath as he stood at his post, back against the door. He was staring at the wall above Lydia, obviously not wanting to make eye contact.

"Lets begin," Mark said, walking over to stand in front of Lydia. They had been through this kind set up before and Caleb took his place behind Lydia facing Mark. Each opened their bibles, closed their eyes and turned their heads up to the heavens. In unison they began the lords prayer in Latin.

"Pater noster qui es in coelis, sanctificetur nomen tuum; adveniat regnum tuum, fiat voluntas tua, sicut in coelo et in terra." The air between them grew warm and a trembling could be felt underfoot. They continued. "Panem nostrum quotidianum da nobis hodie, et dimitte nobis debita nostra," incomprehensible murmurs had started to come from Lydia. Mark looked down at her and while the sounds were definitely issuing from her, Lydia didn't move a muscle. "sicut et nos dimittimus debitoribus nostris." Mark faltered in unease as Lydia smiled at him. Caleb also stopped hearing Mark hesitation.

"What's the matter father?" Lydia said in voice far too aged and dry for her young frame, "Performance anxiety? It happens to every man at some point. Don't worry." She laughed as she stared briefly at his crotch. The laugh was a wretched wound in the silence. Several drowning voices gurgling their glee at once. "Let me finish for you. Et ne nos inducas in tentationem sed libera nos a malo." Both men clutched their ears as Lydia delivered the final word which boomed in every corner of the room. "Amen." The look she gave Mark put him in mind of a wolf tracking its prey. The analogy was made all the more real by the light playing on her irises. He took a breath and composed himself. She had become statuesque once more. Unmoving and cold. He motioned for Caleb to join him in the corner of the room.

"I don't like this," Mark admitted to Caleb in hushed tones, "I'm going to lead prayer, you follow. Don't stop for anything. As much as I hate to admit it, we could be dealing with a genuine case."

"I don't know what's more surprising, Hearing you admit that, or how long its taken you to admit it," Caleb said with a raised eyebrow, realising for the first time that he'd believed from the moment they stepped foot in the hospital. Mark sighed heavily.

"I still want to be absolutely certain." He took another deep calming breath and walked back over the Lydia, not making eye contact with the effigy in the seat that observed them. He nodded at Caleb and began, "Glory be to the Father." Caleb joined in.

"And to the Son, and to the Holy Spirit," Lydia also joined in but in an unknown language.

"As it was in the beginning, is now, and ever shall be, world without end." They ended in unison, "Amen." Undeterred Mark ploughed straight into another prayer.

"Hail Mary full of grace." Caleb quickly joined in.

"The lord is with thee." Again Lydia joined the prayer in another language, maybe Russian. More than that though, it was another voice. She sounded like a old weather-beaten woman. The priests continued.

"Blessed are thou among women, and blessed is the

fruit of thy womb, Jesus. Holy Mary, Mother of God, pray for us sinners, now and at the hour of our death." This time the "Amen." Sounded like a small congregation of disembodied voices. Caleb could see the frustration in Mark's face as he launched into another prayer.

"Blessed be God. Blessed be his holy name." Caleb tried to join in but words wouldn't leave his mouth. By the look of Mark's face he was experiencing the same thing as he stopped and almost choked on his own tongue. Lydia's head had dropped, chin to chest. A voice issued from her that made all four men go pale and the forced the two priests to retreat back from the bound woman.

"Blessed be the bastard son of a vindictive spirit. Blessed be the whore mother and her well ploughed field. Blessed be the shit stained insects that call themselves humanity. And blessed by the hypocrites in charge." At the last line her head swung up to look Caleb dead in the eye, "Of course you know all about hypocrisy don't you, you little fag. Hoping that your big daddy bear protector there will take you into his bed." The gap toothed grin she produced sent a shiver through Caleb's core. "Sorry to disappoint you fairy, but he only likes the ladies." She turned her withering stare on Mark, "Maybe ladies is a bit of a stretch eh Mark?" she winked at him, "How many young girls have you fucked exactly? Five? Ten?" In a flash of movement, Mark was stood again in front of Lydia with a raised hand.

"You shut your fucking mouth!" he screamed at her as his palm connected with her face. The slap sent her head snapping back. Gary was on him in a flash, restraining him and escorting him from the room. The only sound

Mark was aware of was the whistling of Caleb's nose. Then, as if to emphasise that, came those three toneless notes, whistling down the corridor behind them and Lydia, chuckling to herself.

"What in the hell do you think you're doing?" demanded Doctor Whiley as he slammed the door of the small room behind him. Gary had dragged Mark in here after restraining him and was still holding the no longer struggling priest's arms behind his back. Caleb stood in the middle of room, mouth open and head moving from one man to another.

"I'm so sorry Felix. I don't know what came over me. I've never... I would never..." Mark shook his head in self admonition.

"For goodness sake man, let him go," Doctor Whiley told Gary, who until now had stood like an unwavering stone warrior with a strength that seemed disproportional to his jovial manner. He let go of Mark and stood back. Mark rubbed at his arms in the places Gary had restrained him. "How dare you," Doctor Whiley pointed a nicotine stained finger at Mark.

"There is no excuse for-"

"You're right!" He cut Mark off, the heat of his anger adding venom to his words. Mark even shrunk back as the doctor took a step towards him. "There is no excuse. She is a patient, she is a subject of investigation for the church and more than anything she is my granddaughter. If you ever lay a hand on her in anger again, I'll kill you myself." His voice was low and dangerous and a small line of spittle ran down his chin from the corner of his mouth.

"Felix," Caleb stepped between the two men with his

hands raised, "I think we all need to calm down." Doctor Whiley took a step back and clasped a hand over his mouth in shock at his own words.

"I can't believe I just said that. You know me Mark, I'm not a violent man. I've never experienced anger like that. It feels unnatural." He was shaking as he examined his own hands. Mark was equally rattled and trembled as he spoke.

"I don't think it can be denied anymore Felix. It is my opinion that Lydia is possessed. Caleb, do you concur?" Caleb nodded his agreement. "Then I will call the diocese tonight and we will start a full exorcism in the morning." That lead weight feeling had returned to Caleb's stomach as they made their way back to their rooms. Maybe it was apprehension. Maybe it was expectation of Mark telling him they would be fasting and praying in preparation. As archaic as the practice seemed, Caleb knew it was one Mark believed in. He hated feeling hungry though and was already planning what snacks he could help himself to after everyone had gone to bed. Maybe he could get Peaches to leave a little something for him if he asked nicely. Mark's mind was firmly on the matter at hand and the phone call he would have to make to the Diocese. As it turned out though, his worry was for nought. He sat in his room, receiver to his ear and ready to explain the situation. It rang, and rang and rang again before the line clicked and a voice which people seem to reserve only for answer phone messages filled his ear.

"Hello, you have reached the telephone number of Father Palmer. I'm afraid I can't come to the phone right now as I am no doubt indisposed somewhere else. If you'd like to leave me a message, I will get back to you as soon as possible. God bless." -beep.

"Kevin its Mark, uh that is Father Eskil. I'm sorry to have missed you again, but not to worry. I'm just calling to let you know that the investigation has proved positive. That is positive in as much as I can confirm a case of possession. Father Kedge and I will be commencing the full rites tomorrow. I pray that it will be over with quickly. You and I both know how these things can drag on. Anyway, if you need us at all, you know where to find us. Thank you. God bless." And he hung up. It was much later than he had thought when he looked at his watch. He checked through his bag. It had been left behind but Gary had kindly fetched it for him, Caleb's too. Everything seemed to be in order. He thought back over the day's events and his own violent outburst. He was glad that he was the senior priest here. An outburst like that could put him in front of a disciplinary board again. Caleb wouldn't say anything though, he was sure of that. It had been more that twenty years since he had last been in any kind of trouble with the church and he had done everything possible to make sure that wouldn't happen again. He wondered whether Felix was right after all. Had the anger been external, put upon them both? He prayed. Firstly for forgiveness, then for strength. Then he slept. Meanwhile Caleb helped himself to a few slices of ham, a wedge of cheese and some orange juice straight from the carton. He felt better.

Gap toothed grins and reflective eyes had plagued Mark's dreams all night. He half woke several times unsure whether the whistling had followed him out of sleep or if it had woken him. It had been a long time since a legitimate exorcism was needed. He was rusty, to be sure, and the knot of anxiety grew tighter. By the time morning broke, he'd had little sleep but determination fuelled him as he showered and readied himself to do battle with evil. He wrapped a towel around him when someone knocked at his door and answered it still dripping wet.

"Oh sorry. Didn't realise I was disturbing you. I'll come back in ten." Caleb stood there staring at Mark's glistening chest hair.

"No its fine, I was just finishing up. Come in." Mark walked back to his bathroom leaving the door ajar so he could more easily talk to Caleb who had taken a seat on the bed. "You're up bright and early." Mark called back into the room.

"Well, early yes. Not so sure about the bright part. Didn't sleep very well." He didn't mention his suspicion that the cheese before bed probably hadn't helped matters.

"I know that feeling. Still, early to rise, early to work." Caleb caught Mark's reflection in the mirror at that point and had a rise of his own which sent his cheeks scarlet. He cleared his throat.

"I saw Felix this morning. He said we're ready to start whenever suits you. He asked if he could sit in again and I told him it wasn't my decision, but I would talk to you."

"I'm afraid I don't think that's a good idea." Mark came out of the bathroom buttoning up his shirt, "I'll have a word with him before we go in. With the diocese wishes and Lydia being his granddaughter, there's every chance he could be disruptive. Of course, I'll be a bit more delicate with my words." He sat and slipped his shoes on, "But it's fine. You leave that to me." Caleb watched Mark as he finished getting ready and they said a small prayer together before making their way down to Lydia. Marcy and Gary were both there along with Doctor Whiley waiting for them to arrive. "Seems we've got reinforcements today," Mark said quietly out of the corner of his mouth to Caleb.

"Good morning gentlemen," Doctor Whiley greeted them. Marcy Grunted and nodded her own greeting.

"Mornin' fellas." Gary offered his own greeting as he wiped a finger on his shirt that had moments before been up his nose.

"Good morning cavalry," said Mark with a smile, "Felix, may I have a word?" He took a few steps back away from Caleb in the direction they had just come from. "In private, if that's okay." Doctor Whiley went to him, flashing a confused look to Caleb as he did. Caleb simply shrugged back. This was for Mark to deal with.

"I hope you don't mind me saying this Father," Gary said conspiratorially to Caleb as he joined the duo, "But I ain't never seen an exorcism before. Not a real one anyway. I'm quite excited." He looked like a child who'd been told they were going to the zoo.

"Well I've only been involved with one myself. It takes a lot of evidence for it to get this far and most cases simply don't measure up. If you're expecting her head to spin round and pea soup to spew out of her mouth, then you might be a bit disappointed." Caleb nudged Gary in the ribs with his elbow at the joke, trying to keep things light.

Again that strange shifting sensation happened under the skin but before Caleb could register it properly they were interrupted.

"What do you mean I can't be in there? Are you insane? She's my granddaughter!" Doctor Whiley looked both confused and angry as Mark took him by the arm and whispered to him as they took several more steps away from the others. Caleb tried to divert Gary and Marcy's attention back to him.

"Remember though the greatest trick the devil ever pulled was to convince mankind he doesn't exist. Evil is full of lies, so whatever you hear in there, don't believe it."

"Baudelaire," Grunted Marcy, taking Caleb by surprise. He nodded in appreciation of her obviously hidden depths.

"Fine! If you're so determined to keep me out then I'll stay out." Doctor Whiley lit a slender cigar in anger and pointed those nicotine stained fingers at Mark. "If you harm my family Mark, you'll be sorry. I'll be watching everything from my office via the security cameras." And with that he stormed off leaving Caleb and the security guards staring at Mark who sighed and collected himself.

"Have you briefed these two on what's going to happen?" Mark said gesturing at Gary and Marcy as he walked over.

"Well I was going to but-"

"Yes yes. Very well." Mark waved off the excuse and turned his attention to the guards. "Now. It's very important that you remain silent while we perform the exorcism. Understand?" Marcy nodded.

"Oh I don't think that'll be a problem," said Gary with

an overconfident grin.

"I mean it. Absolute silence," Mark clarified, "You may well hear and see things that you wont believe. But unless one of us expressly asks for your help, you are to remain silent. We are about to begin a battle of wills. We need to find the demon's name and then cast it out and back into the pits of hell. Its not for the feint of heart. If you need a few minutes to prepare yourselves, then may I suggest you do it now."

"Well I don't know about collecting myself, but I could do with a piss and a smoke. Be back in five?" Gary was already putting a cigarette to his lips as he and Marcy walked off.

"Are you trying to scare them?" asked Caleb.

"No point sugar coating it Caleb. The last thing we need is an over excited security guard overstepping their bounds and interfering. I'd have them standing watch outside the room if Felix hadn't insisted they be inside" - Mark rummaged in his bag - "Do you have the Eucharist? I can't seem to find any in my bag." They spent the next few minutes double checking their equipment while they waited for Gary and Marcy to return. It was Marcy who opened the door when everyone was ready. The room was cool and the air was stale. Daylight streaming in through the large window behind her threw Lydia's face into shadow. Under the lank grubby hair, the silver eyes could be seen, wide and studying the four people who entered. Nothing else about her moved. They were hard pressed even to see her breathing.

"You take positions by the door. Remember what we said," Mark told Gary and Marcy, as Caleb unpacked his bag onto the table in preparation. Mark's footsteps echoed on the wooden floor as he walked over to his partner. The sound filled the silence of the room. Caleb lit the incense and laid candles about the room while Mark readied himself. "Be sure to lower that blind." Mark pointed at the window behind Lydia. Caleb untied the cord for the Venetian blind but it wouldn't fall. He tried the shutters either side of the window but neither would budge. He stepped away scratching his head.

"I can't get th-" the sound of metal strips crashing down behind him made him jump around as the blind unfurled itself. Even Marcy jumped at the sudden sound and everyone watched the motes of dust travel through the bars of light afforded by the gently swaying blind. Lydia whistled. Mark and Caleb lit the candles. The combination of candlelight along with the incense perfuming the air made the place feel more like a church. With out a word they each took the same positions they had the day before. Mark began the lords prayer.

"Pater noster qui es in coelis." Caleb chanced a glance at Lydia, waiting for the demon to join in again. But there was nothing. She was still. "Sanctificetur nomen tuum. Adveniat regnum tuum. Fiat voluntas tua. Sicut in coelo et in terra. Panem nostrum quotidianum do nobis hodie. Et dimette nobis debita nostra. Sicut et nos dimittimus debitoribus nostris. Et en nos induces in tentationem sed libera nos a malo. Amen."

"Amen," repeated all but Lydia.

"Father Kedge," said Mark, "If you would." At this Caleb nodded and took a silver aspergillum from his pocket. He walked around Lydia's chair flicking holy water from it onto the floor around her while Mark recited the hail Mary. "Hail Mary, full of grace, the Lord is with thee." Some of the holy water hit Lydia's skin, hissing as it did and leaving a small red welt. By the time Mark had got to "and at the hour of our death. Amen." She had several welt across her arms. The final one hissing as the rest of them repeated the Amen. Lydia remained still throughout. Caleb looked at Mark with confusion. This wasn't how it was supposed to go. "Tell me your name demon!" Mark yelled into the silence. Caleb had been standing beside Mark but now took a step back. Lydia looked up now at Mark.

"Demon is it?" came a guttural voice from Lydia. She smiled that gap toothed smile. A whistle came from behind him. Just Caleb's nose. He shuddered slightly and straitened his back in authority.

"That's right. Demon. Foul spirit. You have invaded this poor girl's body and mind. Tell us your name!" His fist tightened around his rosary. Caleb swallowed hard. Lydia laughed.

"Oh you poor little man. Foul spirit indeed. That's rich." The voice smoothed out into something more melodic. Serpentine almost. The sound of it seemed to wrap around the room. Still those unblinking eyes reflected silver light at the priests. "You think you have any power over me, and why? Because of your God?" the room filled with the laughter of a dozen voices, "Let me tell you about your god. Nothing more than a sand spirit taking credit for the acts of other more impressive creatures. Demonising us, literally, and feeding on the poor pathetic humans gullible enough to believe it. There are those of us far older than your God."

"Quiet! You will listen demon!" shouted Mark. He was cut short by the room plunging into darkness as the heavy shutters closed over the window behind Lydia, the force of its movement blowing out all the candles. Still those eyes shone in the darkness.

"No," came a dreamlike voice from everywhere in the room, "It is time for you to listen." The candles all sparked to life and there stood Lydia with a gap toothed grin and no longer restrained. Both priests stepped back in shock and right into vice like grips. Gary and Marcy had moved in silence and now held a struggling priest each on their arms. Their blank faces not even registering pain as Caleb and Mark kicked against them. In a fit of self preservation Caleb bit Gary. The flesh beneath the skin shifted under tooth. Caleb tore into the skin which ripped easily. A granular feeling in his mouth made him spit and splutter as he looked down at the wound. Sand and sawdust spilled from the hole in Gary's arm. "Well now. That wasn't very nice. I don't break your toys." Lydia stood nose to whistling nose with Caleb, who was frozen with fear. "My turn." Before Caleb could blink Lydia had reached up and snapped his neck. "Put him over there." She pointed to the corner of the room and Gary took Caleb's body there silently. Mark looked as all pretence of humanity drained from the stuffed corpse that had once been Gary. He looked even more like a potato sack as he lumbered over and laid his friends body on the floor. The Gary puppet took a few steps back and with a wave of Lydia's hand he collapsed in on himself. "I hate fixing broken toys," she said offhand.

"What have you done! What have you done?!" Mark was pale-faced.

"I told you, it's time for you to listen." Hissed Lydia in a low growl. "You want my name? I've had so many. Barong. Zabaniyya. Leyak. Kara Iye. Astaroth. To most I am simply the shadow that follows," That choral laugh came again, "You humans and your need to name everything. To understand. It's cute really. Pointless, but cute." She squeezed his cheeks like a grandmother with a child. Then slapped him hard across the face.

"What do you want?" Mark asked through gritted teeth.

"Want? I don't want anything. I'm merely the facilitator." Mark looked into those reflective eyes in confusion. "If someone asks for my help in the right way and is willing to pay the price, then I might be inclined to help." Lydia stood back and gave a theatrical bow.

"Are you telling me someone made a deal with you demon?" He asked in surprise. Lydia smirked, "Who?"

"Ah! Finally. A relevant question." She stood back and convulsed into several unnatural poses before raising her head to look at Mark. The reflective silver eyes were now their natural blue.

"Lydia?" Mark asked tentatively.

"That's right Father. Or should I say daddy?" Mark felt a sharp pain in his neck and turned to see Doctor Whiley extracting a now empty syringe from his neck.

"Sleep old boy," He said in a fading voice as Mark slipped into a dreamless void.

Voices came to him in the darkness as he slowly regained consciousness. Not directed at him, just the sounds of conversation fading in and out. Slowly his senses returned in a foggy haze. He quickly realised that he was blindfolded. He tried to swallow and felt a hard plate against his tongue and some contraption stopping his head from moving. He wasn't sure whether the taste of metal was from the thing in his mouth or blood. He couldn't move anything but flexed and moaned against a series of restraints.

"Looks like someone has finally decided to join us. Hello sleepy head," said Lydia. The world was suddenly flooded with light and came into focus as she tugged off the sack that had been covering his head. It took him a moment to get his bearings. The library. He was strapped to the sturdy wooden chair Lydia had been strapped to; the restraints so secure that he couldn't move an inch.

"Good to have you back old boy" - Doctor Whiley lit a cigar and poured himself a whiskey - "I was so hoping to see the look in your eyes before I head off and leave you in your daughter's very capable hands." Mark strained to speak. "Save yourself the effort. Those branks are on nice and tight. Here, see for yourself." He held up a large mirror and Mark could fully see the metal cage that had been placed around his head. A piece of it protruded inward and into his mouth to prevent him from moving his tongue. His shirt had also been ripped open at the front and he could see fine symbols had been cut into his skin. They stung as he traced the lines with his eyes. "All these years and you thought I didn't know you had-" Doctor Whiley swallowed hard, "Relations, with my underage daughter."

"Call it what it is grandpa," She turned her attention to

Mark, "You fucked a little girl. She came to you for
spiritual advice and you raped her." Doctor Whiley
turned away. "And if that wasn't enough you turned her
away when she told you she was pregnant, you killed her
daddy." She spat in his face. "You see I was raised hearing
stories of evil Father Eskil. You were the boogie man of my
childhood. Grandpa told the church. Of course he did.
Why else would you be brought before the council the
way you were. But despite all those other girls they knew
about, all they did was move you to a different parish.
Typical cover up."

"Even when I tried to ruin your good name in a paper
they simply changed your name and ousted me from
future involvement." Doctor Whiley downed his whiskey,
"I promised myself that things would be different with
Lydia." He put a loving hand on her shoulder.

"I however, wanted revenge. Every time someone at
school gave me that look of pity for not having a mother
or father. Every time someone found out my mother had
been underage and committed suicide. I vowed that I
would find a way to punish you. I wanted the world to
know that it wasn't her fault." She beat at her chest in
anger. She stood and smoothed her blouse, "Then when I
was nineteen I had a horse riding accident. The throw put
me in a coma for five days. I wish I could say I don't
remember it but I remember every second. I was in a void,
scared and alone. Around me were voices of all kinds
talking all at once. I thought I had gone mad. After a
while, locked in that state I started to be able to fix on a
single voice for a moment, then another. They say that if a
person dies with unfinished business then they return as a

ghost. That's what I was hearing, the unfinished business, the explanations and excuses. But not all the voices were human. There were others too. I recovered well enough when the coma broke, minus these three teeth of course." She smiled at him showing the false teeth by wiggling them with her tongue. The same ones that created that gap toothed grin that had haunted his dreams. "I decided to dedicate my life to telling those stories. I searched all over the world for the ways and means to do it. Shamanic rituals, gas filled caves of prophecy, Ouija boards. They all have their uses but they weren't good enough. It was at a dig site in Yemen that things started to fall into place. I was researching the prophesies of a young woman who had continued to speak after she had been mummified. The body was long gone of course but that lead me to an obscure reference to 'the shadow that follows'. Naturally I followed the trail and after some time deep in the black forest I found-"

"Me." The voice came from the corner of the room behind Mark. His blood ran cold at the voice and the whistle through a broken nose. "Thanks for the new home Lydia. Its suits me quite nicely." Said the creature wearing Caleb's body as it stepped into view. It grinned at Mark with a familiar smile, but the eyes reflected back silver light. It peeled the cast off of Caleb's nose and stretched out making the neck crack as the bones snapped back into place. "Much better. Such a tight little frame." It slapped its own buttocks with a loud clap. "Oh yes. This will be fun." Mark moaned in protest. "Oh do be quiet. He was already done with it. I couldn't let it go to waste." It stood next to Lydia and faced Mark. "You see even in my stone prison I could feel her anger and need. I just nudged her in the right direction towards a mutually beneficial arrangement." He whistled those three notes.

"My friend here has been around for a very long time. They had been posing as a travelling merchant when they helped the young girl in Yemen get her wish of prophecy. The locals though condemned her for unnatural magic and mummified her alive," Lydia explained.

"So short sighted they were. As if mummifying her would stop her. Some stories are too important," Caleb reminisced, "When the voices from her body were too much to bear, they took her out to sea and dropped her into the depths tied to a rock."

"They also trapped our friend here in a stone pot and sent him to the ends of the earth. Although he hasn't told me how they managed that."

"Nor will I," He smirked back with a cocked eyebrow, "Even locked away as I was, I was able to encourage a group of wolves to make a meal of my would-be transporters and I was dropped in the forest and lost to time. Hardly the ends of the earth but close enough."

"When I finally found the vessel I opened it. There was nothing inside. Or so I thought. That evening my field-guide Brandon came to me."

"Or rather I went to her wearing Brandon. As thanks for helping me I would help her. She could document and tell all the stories she wanted. We just needed the right vessel." They both looked at Mark with a mix of hunger and amusement. He moaned again and tried to flex against the restraints. Nothing moved.

"You were surprisingly easy to snare," said Doctor

Whiley draining another whiskey, "Luther was in prison only a stone's throw from Cambridge. Easy enough to for Lydia to visit and pass along our friend. Once he was in our care, we made it look as convincing as we could. You'll be happy to know we drew inspiration from some of our old investigations. The Prentice boy in particular." Lydia lifted the corner of a cloth covering a medical equipment tray and held up a pair of dental extraction pliers.

"These came in very handy to join the dots between the patients. It was shame about Marcy and Gary. I liked them, but they were the first to go. Collateral damage you understand. Our friend found a use for them though after a bit of modifying." Mark thought about the sand and sawdust under Gary's skin. "As strong as Luther seemed, he was actually quite weak. His blood made such pretty patterns though." She stroked the pliers and placed them back on the tray.

"I almost felt sorry for Reece when I was in him," continued the creature in Caleb's skin, "Pitiful man. Didn't appreciate what he had. All his problems were made by his own hand. Still there's nothing quite like the feel of a noose." Caleb shivered with what looked like pleasure.

"I dispatched Father Palmer myself," said Doctor Whiley, "Simply let myself into his house and stabbed him through the heart. His own punishment for not dealing with you when he had the chance. Then I sent you the files and diverted his voicemail."

"Hello, you have reached the telephone number of Father Palmer," It was Kevin's voice coming from Caleb. His smile widened, "I'm afraid no one knows where you are Mark." Mark's eyes filled with tears as he realised how hopeless the situation was.

"Don't cry daddy. You're going to help me. More than you know," said Lydia removing the cover completely from the tray of surgical instruments, "In fact, you're going to help all of those lost voices that need to be heard." She picked up a scalpel.

"Uh uh!" said Caleb, "Payment first. That's the deal. A willing sacrifice."

"Of course," she agreed, "Grandpa?" He drained his third whiskey and took a large drag on his cigar before stubbing it out in the cut glass ashtray.

"I'm ready," he said, standing with his eyes closed. Caleb walked over to him and whispered something in his ear. Doctor Whiley was trembling and turned white as a sheet.

"Sealed with a kiss," Caleb said as he leaned in and locked lips with the old man, holding onto his frail skull as he sucked the life out of him. He dropped the doctors corpse to the floor with a thud. He groaned with satisfaction and blew out a wisp of cigar smoke.

"What a shame," said Lydia looking at her crumpled grandfather, "Still he said he'd do anything for me. Now its your turn daddy." Mark tried squirming again, the look of fear clear on his face. "Oh don't worry, no kisses for you. We need you alive. Remember the poor mummified girl in Yemen? She was just a vessel for communication. An Oracle of flesh. Now it's your turn. You see, here's a fun fact I learnt from Grandpa. Spirit voices don't come from the mouth. They come from the throat. In fact I think you taught him that. So I'm afraid it looks like the branks are staying. How then do we get the sound out of your throat?" She pondered out loud as she tapped the tip of a scalpel against a false tooth. "Of course," she held the blade in front of her in mock realisation. Mark felt Caleb's hands clamp down on his shoulders from behind. Caleb was muttering under his breath, an incantation of some sort. Lydia positioned herself in front of her father and stared at his bare neck. She raised the blade to a point above his Adam's apple and punctured the skin. Mark tried to squirm, to move against the pain but was powerless to stop as she made the incision down the length of his throat. He could feel the blood trickle down his bare chest and across the raised symbols inscribed there. She took pieces of steel cable from the tray and threaded them through each edge of the incision. She pulled back the wires and secured them to hooks in the wood of the chair which Mark could not see. The exposed flesh bobbed up and down as he tried to swallow away the pain. She took the scalpel again and swiftly opened up a small hole above the Adams apple, avoiding the vocal chords. Voices whispered up from the hole that were not Mark's. Each sound feeling like a grain of salt on the raw opening of his neck. Lydia took a step back to admire her work. "Oh its perfect," she said sounding like a giddy schoolgirl, "He wont die will he?" Caleb released Mark's shoulders and came to inspect Lydia's handy work.

"Very nicely done," he said satisfied, "And no, he wont die. The spell means he will be around for a very very long time. In fact it could be generations." Tears rolled down Mark's face. "I believe our deal is done my dear. I will leave you to your research."

"Will I see you again?" she asked hopefully.

"Oh I'm always around. You can count on it." And he strode out of the library. Those three tuneless whistles echoing down the corridor as he left the asylum. Lydia took a seat at her desk facing Mark. Opening a drawer she took out a leather notebook and Mark's Dictaphone. She filled a glass with whiskey from the bottle her grandfather had never finished. Clicking the Dictaphone to record, she looked admiringly at her Oracle.

"So. Who wants to tell me a story?"

STORY TWO
Cold Water

Evidence Submission Tango-Delta-One. Crow Wing County sheriff's department.

Description : Brown, leather bound journal. Approximately 9x14 centimetres. Found in the stored belongings of the suspect's father, a mister Buddy Keefer, deceased, 4 years ago. Suspect, Michael Keefer, is still missing. Below is the transcript of a journal belonging to the late Buddy Keefer. Transcribed, where possible, by deputy James Thorson.

I fear that I may soon be taken to face my final judgement. I'm no longer able to do what is demanded of me. Now as the snow builds higher in the streets, I know that debts must be paid one way or another. I cannot beg forgiveness for what I have done, nor will I. My only hope is that this never comes to light, but for the sake of my own sanity, I have to explain.

I was just a teenager when my father died. We lived then, as I still do, in Garrison, which is on a bay of the Mille Lacs lake. The perfect place for a boat builder like dad to live. To live and to die. Of course, being the stone hearted son of a bitch that I'd known growing up, people didn't mourn him for very long. Myself included. You see my father had been grouchy at best and a down right terror at worst. My mother had died when I was just four years old, leaving me in his sole care. He had no other living family so I spent most of my time with the neighbours. Too many times did I have to hide the welts he had left from the previous day's beating with a belt. It was never anywhere people would see of course, only ever where clothes would cover the red and purpling streaks left by the strap. I'm sure several of the neighbours knew but they where too afraid to say anything. The best times of my childhood were in the deep winter when he would go off hunting for a week or more at his cabin the woods. He never bought back anything of significance, maybe a few ducks. But I was too happy in his absence to question it.

At fifteen I started working as a carpenter's apprentice. Living for so long with a boat builder, even a bully like my dad, you pick up a few things about woodworking. I was a natural and enjoyed the smell of timber and the feel of the grain under my hands as I worked the rough hewn planks into all manners of furniture and boxes. I think in his way my dad was also proud of me. My family had always worked with wood, either building boats like dad or barrels like my grandfather and his father before him. So while he still wasn't pleasant to be around, at least we had common ground and I could tolerate dad. Just a year after I started working for him, my boss Michael Hurley employed me full-time and set me up with an area in his workshop of my own, for me to do with as I pleased. He'd even given me a small bonus to buy something just for me. He knew nearly all my wages were taken by my dad. I took the money and bought myself a deep red Bakelite Farnsworth radio to sit among the pots of varnishes and lacquers in my new work area. Rock and roll now filled the air along with the sawdust.

On my seventeenth birthday, I was at the shop and working on an antique cabinet for the local bed and breakfast. Every summer saw groups of tourists come to Garrison bay to take row boats out onto the water. Summers here were a far cry from the freezing winters and the ice fishing that followed. But this year a heatwave had seen a record number of visitors. Many had to camp in the woods as all the rooms for rent had been taken. Now that the late September chill had settled in and the tourists left, a discussion had been prompted among the community as to whether more investment in tourism was needed. As you are probably aware from the town now, tourism has become a booming industry of its own. While I was crouching in the jaws of the cabinet, its broken hinged door the victim of a particularly rowdy group of tourists, I heard Mr Hurley say "Jack! Its nice to see you." There was no response but I knew all too well the look that would be on my father's face that kept Mr Hurley from pursuing the conversation. I took my head out and turned the volume down on Buddy Holly, my favourite artist, as my father entered my area of the workshop.

"Dad," I said, with a nod at the long item roughly wrapped in brown paper under his arm, "What brings you here?"

"Birthday present," he half grunted. He looked thin and

pale. The last couple of years had not been kind to him and he seemed to age quickly. He'd recently developed a nervous tick too. An odd jerk of his head every now and then. He handed me the parcel and I pulled away the brown paper to reveal a hunting rifle underneath. "I thought since I was too ill to go hunting last year, you might want to join me this year. You know, now you're old enough to be responsible for yourself." That nervous tick again. It put me on edge. The decline in his health started with last years influenza that had put him in bed for over a month. Maybe his yearly hunt could get him back on his feet and breathe some fresh life into him. I suspected he just needed me their because he still wasn't feeling a hundred percent. Whatever the reason, I agreed. Besides, it was still a few months away yet. He'd probably change his mind.

December came and by the middle of the month the lake had frozen over. The streets were being hand-cleared of snow twice a day and my father and I were packing warm clothes and hunting equipment. It would be a day's trek to his little cabin in the woods. I'd never seen it before so I was excited that he was sharing this part of his life with me.

"When we get there I have so much to show you," he said with that unnerving tick of his. It was now present most of the time. It was good to see him smile and be excited, but at the same time my stomach churned in anticipation. Before sunrise, we had set off. My father insisted we do no hunting on the way, instead wanting to set up a base camp at the cabin and go out from there. We stopped twice to sparingly eat the light provisions we had ready. "We'll catch more while we're up there and there are plenty of canned goods at the cabin if we need them," he assured me. Despite how frail he looked, he had guided us unerringly to the small wooden shack deep in the woods. Even after walking all day and seeing the sun set, he knew exactly where to go and we arrived safely. Inside was cold and dark but he walked straight in and with the strike of a match lit an oil lantern. The floors and walls were decorated with pelts of all kinds of animals. There was a small pot bellied stove in the middle of one wall and a stack of dry wood next to it. He took several pieces and easily lit the stove to warm the cosy space.

"Where are the beds?" I asked.

"There" - he pointed at two piles of blankets, rags and furs each in their own corners - "We can make a pallet each out of those."

"And the tinned food?" I asked, none to happy about the sleeping arrangements. He stamped on the floor three times, sending up thick motes of dust that swirled in the firelight of the lantern and stove.

"Root cellar," he said without looking up from the fire he was coaxing into even larger flames, "Take this." He took a foil wrapped sandwich from his pack beside the fire and threw it to me with another of those nervous ticks. "We've got an early start tomorrow, so get some sleep." I couldn't tell if he was smiling or grinning but my stomach churned again and not just because of the smell of tuna sandwiches.

I woke the next morning to find him staring at me from his own pallet on the other side of the room. The fire had died back leaving only a glow in the room which reflected off the eyes looking straight at me.

"Ready to go?" he asked.

"Dad, let me wake up a bit," I said, sitting up and shaking the sleep from my head.

"Early hunter catches his prey." The turn of phrase unsettled me for some reason as I got up and dressed ready for the day. Dad was already dressed under the pelt he had over him and was ready to go straight away. We left the cabin in the pre-sunrise darkness and I followed him closely to wherever he was leading us. We'd walked for a couple of hours and still the sun hadn't risen.

"How much further dad? And how early is it?" I asked. My knees were protesting at the cold walk but he was still going strong.

"Early?" he said with a chuckle. "It's not early. It's late. You slept all day. It must be coming up to midnight now."

"What?! How can that be?"

"It happens," he said, turning back to face me briefly with a grin on his face. He looked like he hadn't slept at all; the low lamplight throwing his face into a sharp relief that frankly unsettled me for a moment. "We're nearly at the water," he said, turning back to the path that only he, in his mind's eye, could see.

'Not ice fishing' I thought. I hated ice fishing. But then again if it made him happy and potentially made him well again, I would do it.

Twenty, or maybe forty, minutes later (it was hard to keep track) we arrived at the edge of the lake. Far from Garrison bay it was a stretch of the shore I didn't know. The water was a thick crust of ice. Its crystalline formations threw back reflected light from the lantern. Beyond the light's circular reach was blackness. My father stepped out onto the ice without breaking stride. His path was set and he was heading straight for his destination. I quickly followed not wanting to be swallowed by the blackness all round us. The wind died down more and more as we walked out onto the ice, instead of picking up as I'd expected it to do. He was a few paces ahead of me when I heard him chuckle to himself as he stopped. I came up beside him and saw ten yards away from us a row boat completely locked in by the ice. Maybe someone had accidentally let it loose from the jetty and it had been lost on the water, freezing here in place. My father walked over to it, stepped in and took a seat.

"You better hurry," he said with a cackle, "It's coming." Just then there was a yawning creak as the ice split somewhere close by. Then another creak on the other side of me. Without thinking I ran the short distance and leapt into the boat. My weight on the ice made several more cracks. A spiderweb of fractures across the surface now radiated from the boat itself. I struggled to think, to breathe. All the while dad just looked at me, unblinking, twitching. Then there was silence. For several heartbeats the world was muted. The boat, now free of its icy restraints, bobbed on the surface along with great shards of frozen lake. Then it came. I could feel it in my guts and along my spine before I heard it. The deepest, most monstrous sound. Like a sleeping giant letting out a long sigh. "It's here. Its always here. And now its coming for you. It told me it needs to take you if I am to be saved. Just like it needed your grandfather."

"What are you talking about?!" I'd barely finished the last word when he lunged at me in a blind rage. I managed to react quickly and moved to pin him to the floor of the boat. Water washed over his laughing mouth which made a wretched gurgling. Just then the boat began to slowly turn round and round in the water. Ice platforms around us started to sink like they were being sucked down under us. They were sliding toward us on the surface before slipping below the edge of the boat and descending into the depths beneath us. The deep monstrous sound came to a crescendo. The noise so loud I had to cover my ears, letting my father go in the process. He leapt to his feet and with one hand around my throat lifted me up and over the edge of the boat, inhuman strength coursing through him. I looked down into the water below and saw a perfectly circular sink hole right below us. But that couldn't be. The lake bed must be a hundred feet or more below us. Yet here, not ten feet below the surface, was a ring of stone with steep sloping sides. In the centre was a seemingly bottomless hole. Its sides were glassy and throwing back the lamp light. Maybe it was hysteria in the moment, but I swear I could see shapes moving inside the smooth walls of the hole. Like faces through frosted glass.

"I have him. I brought him for you!" A bubble of foul smelling gas broke the surface next to the boat, rocking it violently. "What do you mean?" he said to the night sky as he dropped me unceremoniously back into the boat. "But, but, I brought him. Like you said." He was rambling and I managed to steady myself in the boat, readying myself in case he attacked me again. The sound had changed around us. Now among the deep guttural noise was a roiling fleshy sound that drew nearer. I could feel it in my skull as much as hear it and my father cursed the water below us then turned his attention to me. "YOU!" he frothed at me, his eyes bulging with rage and fear, "They need to take you. It has to end with me!"

The water erupted around us in white foam. It blinded us both as it splashed around us and in our eyes. Through the distortion, I could make out horrendous shapes, darker than the night sky, whipping back and forth. The sound split the air. The squelching fleshiness of it, along with the smell of rotted fish, made me gag. Then he started screaming. I put out my arm to reach him and he tore my right sleeve clean off as the monstrosity lifted him into the air. I could hear the rending of flesh and his scream died with a gurgle. Quick as a flash, the whole writhing mass withdrew back into the water, taking his mutilated corpse with it.

It took several minutes to clear my eyes and for the water to calm enough to lean over the boats edge. The hole seemed to be shrinking, retreating slowly back into the deep. I heard my dads voice, or thought I did. Looking down I could see his face, like a spectre in the walls of the hole. I reached into the water without thinking and something grabbed my wrist. A sticky tendril of some kind that stung me. It released me just as quickly and I fell back into the boat. Unconscious.

I was found two days later. Barely alive and floating in a large area of cracked ice. I was taken to the state hospital where I was in a coma for fourteen months. Having no other living relatives, Mr Hurley took full responsibility for me. When I eventually woke, I had no brain damage and could remember everything up until the morning we left home to go hunting. I had lost two toes to frostbite and had two circular patches of white skin on my right wrist, also frostbite I was told. When I was strong enough to start asking questions, the sheriff gave me a full breakdown of what they thought had happened. My fathers body had been found a little way into the woods, savaged by a bear. They figured that the bear had surprised us with it being hibernation season and had attacked. I must have run out onto the ice in panic and found the boat. It seemed to make sense. My fathers house and the business were now mine. The house is the same house I live in now. The boat shop I sold and bought a partnership with Michael Hurley. Somewhere along the way I had lost my sense of humour. It was put down to grief by some, traumatic stress by most. It was like my emotions had been robbed from me. I felt cold inside.

As the winter winds began to blow through Crow Wing county, the marks on my wrist began to itch. I woke several night in succession in cold sweats clutching the wrist with my other hand. I had night terrors which I couldn't remember in waking but felt so real in the moment. Whilst I was working I would hear odd whispers that seemed to come from nowhere. Only the radio could drown it out. Michael noticed the change in me the most. One night I woke with a scream, sweating and clutching my wrist. The tingling felt fresh and everything came back to me in one glorious and monstrous wave of nightmare. I remembered everything. The snow was falling outside but

I had to talk to someone. I dressed quickly and walked to Michael's house. He being a confirmed bachelor, I knew I would only be waking him. Bleary eyed, he invited me in and poured us each a warming brandy as I told him the whole bloody story. He took my shaking hands in his.

"My dear boy. It's just stress. It's been such an overwhelming time for you. Your brain has obviously taken some old native myth and mixed it with an awful memory to help you cope."

"Native myth?" I asked.

"Of course, the um... oh hell and damnation I can never remember. But it's the lake monster, like Loch Ness but less friendly. It's just their way of keeping people off the ice in winter. You know how many accidents there are every year. Come with me." He stood up and put on a heavy long coat. "We're going down to the bay. Seeing how clear it is will put your mind at rest." I didn't think, I just followed. We walked to the iron gates of the newly built visitors' dock. It was quiet and still. Michael was talking about how many tourist there were these days. I wasn't really listening. My wrist felt like I'd been stung by a frozen hornet. A pressure was building in my chest and head that made my vision blurry. "What's that?" Michael asked. Then I heard it, that deep yawning. It was coming, and I was running on auto pilot. Aware but not in control. I grabbed Michael, pushing his arm up his back as I clamped my other hand over his mouth. I frogmarched him to the end of one of the jetties and sure enough, down below was that smooth round opening. I threw him in to the waiting tendrils without a thought and turned away, walking calmly home. The next day his body was found frozen to a Park bench like he'd simply sat and been taken by the cold. Whatever this thing was it had made both my father's and Michael's deaths seem like accidents. My emotions never really broke the surface. Inside I was dying.

By spring I had decided to find someone native and ask about the myth of the lake monster. I was sure I'd never heard anything about it before the coma, as Michael had suggested. It stood to reason though that, whatever this monster is, they must know something. Everyone I tried to speak to turned me away. A wall of silence at every enquiry, until eventually I heard about and tracked down an outcast shaman known as the Crowman of Crow Wing county. He was living up-state in a makeshift camp of broken down RV's. It took me three months of searching the forest before I found the ring of vehicles. It was a welcome sight. I entered the clearing between two rusted mechanical hulks that were as much protective wall as living spaces.

"You found us," came a voice from the darkened doorway of an adjacent camper.

"Us?" I asked, "I was told the Crowman lives alone."

"He does," came the chuckling reply, "But who says the others here are living." He stepped from the shadows and stood with his arms folded across his chest. His piercing stare was unsettling. "Not what you were expecting eh?" He was right. I had been picturing an old native man. Feathers, tanned leather and suede, the whole nine yards. Instead I was standing just ten yards from this thirty-something dark skinned man. Clad in denim and leather.

He looked more like a biker than a shaman. "Come and warm yourself by the fire. Night is coming and I fear our conversation isn't fit for the daylight." He was right, the sun was starting to dip towards the horizon and the wind outside the camp's protection carried a biting chill. We sat across from each other with the fire between us as he stoked the flames. He clicked his tongue and hummed a tune while he sprinkled sage and other herbs onto the fire which filled the area with an earthy perfume.

"Why do you live out here all alone?" I asked him. He cocked his head a little and seemed to be looking through me.

"My mother was a shamaness of the Ojibwe people. She was guided in a vision to help a man in need. A Haitian man who was being hunted by people who wanted to hang him. Luckily she found him in time and guided him to safety, saving his life in the process. That man was my father, a shaman of his own kind. Against the wishes of her people, they fell in love. From that love I was born. It was clear from a young age I would also be shaman, having gifts from both my parents. They taught me all they could but the rest of our community were afraid of me. Of course to start with, it was just the colour of my skin, but as I got older and started conversing with the dead, a gift I inherited from my father, other fears came forwards. I gave them warnings of floods and droughts, interpreted dreams and tried to be as helpful as I could. Still they were afraid. The three of us lived at the edge of the community until a few years ago. A great illness came across the land and many died, my parents included. There were whispers among some people of my being responsible for the sickness. So before they could act, I left." I was transfixed by his voice. I don't think he blinked once while he spoke. Then it was like a spell had broken and he relaxed a little closing his eyes. "But you are not here to talk about me." He opened his eyes and fixed his gaze on me again.

"You're right. But I'm not really sure where to begin. The whole thing sounds so crazy." I was shaking now and trying desperately not to stumble nervously over my own words.

"Just take a deep breath. Let the herbs calm you. You are in a safe space. Now begin." So I did. Once I started I couldn't stop. It spewed forth from me almost involuntarily. I told him about my dad, the hunting trip, the lake, the way dad died, the coma, Michaels death and my hand in it, the nightmares, my emotionless responses to it all. Each piece of the story told felt like I was unburdening myself.

"And that's all of it," I said slumping into my seat deflated and shaking my head. The Crowman looked grey. His eyes narrowed and pale. Beads of sweat had broken out across his brow. "Are you okay?" I asked. He stared blankly for a few seconds then cleared his throat.

"What I am about to tell you is the truth behind the legend." He leaned closer to the fire, his face framed in flame as he spoke. "It is true that there are legends about sea serpents and lake monsters all over the world. Cautionary tales about the deep water. The lake you call Mille Lacs has another name, a much older and secret name. A name that translates to 'Spirit lake'. It is said to be a gateway to a realm of unspeakable horrors. The story says that a small tribe of cursed medicine people used to guard the water and feed a great beast. Other tribes would stay far away from them for fear of being sacrificed. They believed that if the beast of the water was kept satisfied, then it would keep the way closed so nothing could pass over from the other side. But it had a price. A toll that the medicine-men paid willingly. The beast would mark the medicine-men and take away their joy and happiness. The lake made them cold inside, to be able to do such a monstrous task. Being bound, as they were, to such a horror made many of them mad. They couldn't close the gateway, so they obeyed. One day a young medicine-man took it upon himself to try to end the curse and banish the beast for good. He believed he had found a way to destroy the gateway. On his way to the waters edge, painted in blood for the ceremony, he encountered a woodsman who was out chopping trees. They startled each other and the woodsman swung his axe, killing the young medicine man. That twist of fate released the tribe of the curse, killing them all in the process. The ritual to close the gateway, lost when the young tribesman died. But the curse, the curse persisted. It was transferred it to the woodsman. Now hearing your story I'm certain that the woodsman was an ancestor of yours. This curse has been being passed down your family. You are the new guardians."

"That's ridiculous! Nonsense!" I stood up holding my head which was now swimming. Quickly he was standing beside me and supporting my weight.

"And yet you know its true," he said softly to me, "Sit. I think maybe I can help you." I sat and he gave me a tin cup of water to sip. "I believe I can perform a ceremony of my own to close the gate for good. It will be very dangerous for me and will take weeks of daily rituals by the water. I will prepare and leave in the morning. You don't have to do anything. If I am successful, you should feel the bond break."

"And if you aren't successful?" I asked.

"Pray to whatever god you believe in that I am." We sat a while more in silence. I drifted into a sleep full of visions of monsters and curses and the thing in the lake. When I awoke, the Crowman was already slinging a large pack over his shoulder and getting ready to set off. "I just need a few things from you," he said, and after collecting blood, spit and hair from me, he wished me luck and we parted ways; me home and him on his journey. The next two nights were fraught with similar nightmares. On the third night I had been sleeping peacefully until a lancing shard of pain in my wrist woke me up. I clutched at the wrist around the marks that had been left there and passed out from the pain. I woke up the following evening to a commotion on the street outside. A man had been found mutilated just one street over surrounded by strange items. Herbs, bones and carved dolls. When I finally pushed through the crowd of onlookers, I could scarce believe my eyes. He was mutilated beyond all recognition, but it was the Crowman. His body was a clear message to me. I would never be free. So I resigned myself to my fate. Over the years, each time the pull became too strong to bear and the voices too loud on my head, I would find a hapless tourist, or gullible passer-by, and take them down to the water's edge to sacrifice them. Their bodies would turn up later, by a way still unknown to me, looking like an accident. Each time made me a little colder and more bitter. It had a control over me which was hard to resist.

They wanted me to have a child. A gifted offspring to carry on after me. It was an itch in my brain I couldn't scratch. I shacked up with a waitress, Judy Horner, who quickly fell pregnant. We had a daughter, Sheryl. A few months later I was drawn to walk along the shore with them both, Sheryl in a stroller. The atmosphere was thick and I could feel Sheryl was under scrutiny. It was made very clear that she was not suitable as Judy was taken by the creature in the lake. She was found the next morning at her restaurant, an apparent brain haemorrhage. Judy's parents took care of Sheryl. It was a couple of years later that I married Linda and shortly after we had Michael. Named after my old boss. Again I was drawn to the water to let it probe at my son. I left Linda at home for fear it would take her too if unsatisfied. The fear was unwarranted. It seemed to approve of Michael. And so life went on. I worked and I provided for my family. When the radio from the shop, which now lived on the windowsill by the kitchen sink, couldn't drown out the voices, then I performed my sacrificial duty. Life went on like this for years.

As Michael got older I started to notice worrying traits in him. He would often wander down to the lake and come back angry for no reason. Occasionally cats would go missing and wind up a few days later drowned by the shore. I started to theorise that maybe whatever the lake was keeping back could still somehow seep through and effect people. The Crowman's description of people going mad rang in my head. It was unnerving to consider the implications and see the effect on Michael, even at such a young age. He reminded me of my father. When I asked him about it, he didn't even remember being by the lake. I tried my best to keep him away from the water and for a few years the distance worked. He was a normal kid who hated his dad for being so hard on him. He went through high school resenting me and I was fine with that. Better he hate me for being a hard-ass than the alternative. In his late teens he started sneaking around. "He's just meeting girls," Linda would say, innocent that she was. It would have broken her heart to know her son was a queer. He always kept away from the water though. I felt safe in the knowledge that he may be a fag, but at least he's not a psychopath. Michael was twenty five when Linda died. Cancer. I was out when it happened, feeding the lake. Michael never forgave me for not being there and for not shedding a tear. I had grown much colder inside now. Amid his rage at me, between shouting and crying, I had a flash of insight, a picture of a future that scared me. I saw Michael in my place carrying the curse. I saw it crush him and I saw him fail. He was the deranged image of my own father. It haunted me as we arranged the funeral and I decided I had to do something to get him as far away as possible from the lake. The day of the funeral I started an argument with him in front of everyone. We went back and forth riling each other up until I called him a liberal queer. Red in the face he snapped back and told me I should be the one in the box at the front. It broke my heart that I couldn't tell him it was for his own good. He left that night for San Francisco and I haven't heard from him since. That was ten years ago. Sheryl still talks to him maybe once every two years. She told him he was an uncle when Jason, her son, was born. Intuitive little guy. Some might even say gifted. Only three years old and he already sees the lake for what it is. He will be a good replacement for me.

I write this with a wrist on fire because I can feel my mind slipping. The creature in the lake is stirring in a way I haven't felt before. I have nightmares of Michael, grinning and covered in blood over the body of a young boy. I fear for Jason. My only hope is to keep Michael away. Thankfully our relationship is strained enough that even with my imminent death he should stay away. He won't grieve for me. The curse will pass to poor Jason. I know he will be able to handle it in time. The voices are calling. The creature wants me. The lake needs me. The water...

Transcript end. The writing becomes illegible from here and devolves into a scrawl accompanied by several unknown symbols. It is the opinion that the notebook contains the fictional writing of a troubled man. After five days neither the alleged kidnapper Michael Keefer, nor the victim Jason Thomas Horner have been found.

STORY THREE
Mothers Help

If you ever find yourself near Crabtree Lane, you'd be best to avoid the policemen near dark alleyways. Of all the corrupt areas of London, Bethnal Green was one of the worst. Crabtree Lane was a dark and overcrowded street right in the middle of it all. The last thing any respectable person would want is to feel the grubby, white-gloved hand of a copper on the take. Eric knew this all too well as he walked the cobbled streets, arm in arm, towards the basement flat of number nine.

"Remember my dear," he said to the woman accompanying him, "You will be playing mother tonight and I am your son Henry. Understand?"

"Yes Eric," she said. He shot her a stern look. "I mean Henry," she corrected, "We're not going to hurt her are we?"

"Of course not. She's only going to get what's coming to her. Now stand up straight." He stopped and brushed dandruff from his fictional mother's shoulders. He used to enjoy much younger assistants, but needs must he thought. In truth, Jane was only ten years his senior, but the application of their disguises had lent more credence to their invented relationship. She was no music hall actress, in fact she was no actress at all, but a secretary. Still she was up to the task of this pantomime. "Don't get drawn in," he warned her, "Say as little as possible and try to remain unnoticed. You can make our introductions, but the rest is up to me." He hooked her arm in his again. "Take a deep breath. We're here." He flourished his hand towards the dank stairway down to their destination. They descended into the smell of damp and mildew. Taking his place behind his 'mother' he reach forward and pulled the lever for the bell. It hung limply, being either broken or disabled. He rapped on the wood of the door. Peeling blue paint stuck to his knuckles in flecks that he wiped off with a fresh hanky. He removed his top hat as footsteps from inside came to the door. The clunk of the latch was followed by a long creak as the door was slowly opened. A young grubby boy greeted them with a somber face. Eric nudged Jane in the back.

"I'm Mrs Drake," she stammered out, "This is my son er..."

"Henry," Eric finished for her, "I believe we are expected." The boy nodded and turned to walk back into the hall, signalling for them to follow. Eric closed the door behind him having a good look around in the oil lamp light as he followed Jane. The boy opened a the second of the two doors in the corridor and stood aside, motioning for them to enter. Jane gasped and Eric was not disappointed as they walked in to the room lit by a single candle at the centre of a large round table. Eleven people sat around the table in total. All with expectant and somber faces. All of them except for the one they had come to see. Madam Kline. She was sat with her hands resting palms up on the table, eyes half closed.

"We've been expecting you," she said. The candle light was reflected in the rings and bangles she wore as well as the beads which adorned the edge of the shawl she had around her head. "Please take a seat and we can begin." They took the two vacant seats and exchanged glances with the other attendees. Some were already weeping. Once everyone was settled Madam Kline took a deep breath in and closed her eyes. The room fell silent as all eyes turned to her. She exhaled, "We gather here, we thirteen, to commune with those who have departed this realm of flesh." Her voice resonated in the small room. The slight hint of an eastern European accent caught Eric's ear. "Everyone link hands and we will begin." The crowd did as they were told. Madam Kline sat back in her chair and turned her head to the ceiling, "Spirits of the hereafter, I call to you. Come to us in our hour of enquiry. Linger with us a while and bring comfort to those of us in need." Without opening her eyes she turned her head in the direction of a young couple to her left. "We have a little visitor," she said to the space between the couple. Her eyes remained closed. "Well then, what is your name young one?" She paused and cocked her head, listening to the blank space. "Well its very nice to meet you Jennifer." The young woman clutched at her face with a lace handkerchief, tears streaming down her cheeks. Her sobs broke the silence as she squeezed the hand of her ashen-faced husband beside her. Madam Kline opened her eyes. "She says she misses you very much mummy and daddy.

But don't be sad. She has lots of friends to play with."

"Marbles?" Asked the young woman between sobs, "She loved playing with marbles. She was even buried with some."

"Yes," said Madam Kline with a smile, "Marbles." At that moment the sound of something small and hard rolled across the floor made the husband jump up. "Please stay seated Mr West. Do not break the circle," she ordered in a stern voice. He took his seat. "You must not worry sir. She says that her aunt Edith is taking good care of her."

"Edith?" he said shocked, "My sister Edith? Is she here too?" Tears now rolling down his cheeks.

"I can only allow one spirit at a time. She may come through later. Is there anything you wish to say to Jennifer?"

"We love you so much," said Mrs West, "So very very much. Are you in pain anymore?"

"No mummy," said Madam Kline in a small girlish voice, "I can breathe properly again." She took a deep breath in and out. "She's beginning to fade now. She wants you to know that it's fine to let her go. She is happy." At that moment a girls laughter emanated from thin air over the table. Everyone looked with shock and awe at each other. "There is another spirit present here." A look of concern crossed Madam Kline's face. "You poor dear," she said facing straight ahead, eyes shut once again. "A young man who was in a terrible accident. A recent death. He has not yet had time enough to heal on the other side. He isn't able to speak yet."

"Oh my goodness," said an older cockney lady across from Madam Kline, "It's my Billy!" Madam Kline took a deep breath.

"Spirit, I invite you to knock on the table if you're able. One knock for yes and two for no. Do you understand?" At that, a single loud knock came from the centre of the table. Several people peered under the tablecloth into the darkness ringed by legs and feet. There was nothing there. "Billy, is that you?" Again a single knock on the table. Billy's mother gasped.

"He was hit by a carriage you see. Mangled. I hoped but never thought he'd appear" colour had drained from the older womans face. Madam Kline opened her eyes and stared at Billy's mother.

"There is something I can try. It might help him come through to speak to you, but its very dangerous and I would need to be compensated for the danger. Is that agreeable?"

"Yes yes, of course. Please try anything."

"Very well. This is very dangerous, as I have said, and I require the utmost silence from everyone. Do not move. Any interruption could kill me." Everyone leaned in closer with baited breath. All except Eric, who was glancing around the rest of the room at the dusty books on esoteric arts, several candle sticks and various knick-knacks. His attention was brought back to Madam Kline when someone in the group gasped. She was sat back in her chair, head thrown back and eyes showing only white. She held her throat as from her mouth a thin tendril of some fluid looking substance had started to snake its way into the air in front of her. Someone in the crowd whispered "ectoplasm" and at that Eric saw his opening. He stood from his place and walked quickly to the door they had entered from. Flinging the door open he quickly grabbed the oil lamp from the hall.

"I'm afraid ectoplasm is far from the truth. In fact ladies and gentlemen, nothing you have seen here tonight has been the truth. Isn't that right?" He pointed a finger at Madam Kline and all eyes turned on the woman who was trying to quickly recover and hide whatever it was that had been issuing forth from her mouth.

"I don't know what you mean, but you are certainly not welcome here sir!"she said in defiance.

"Of course you know. You see ladies and gentlemen, Madam Kline the great European mystic and seer does not exist."

"Now see here," said Mr West, "What on earth do you think you're playing at? She's right there. Who are you too besmirch this good woman's name?"

"Good woman?" laughed Eric, as he walked around the room lighting the candles, "My dear fellow, I doubt she will ever be called that again. I however am Eric White of the Illustrated London News."

"Eric White the magician," said the woman accompanying Billy's mother, "I saw you some twenty years back. Must've been 1883 at the Empire. I didn't know you was a reporter now."

"Indeed I am." He bowed to the group and took his place standing behind the still seated Madam Kline. "I report on murder and mystery. The latter of which I use my not inconsiderable knowledge of deception to unmask charlatan mediums. You see ladies and gentlemen, this is not Madam Kline. This is Anna Clune. Mother of three and wife of a convicted murderer." They all gasped. Now in full light they could see that this middle aged woman was in fact no older than 30. Her appearance had been made older with the use of dirt and ash. She stared stone-faced at the wall opposite, not making eye contact with anyone. "And what exactly was your ectoplasm my dear? Tissue paper and egg whites?" she struggled against him as he took her wrist and produced a material from a crudely painted flesh coloured tube secured beneath the bangles. "Ah, cheesecloth" - he held up the evidence - "A classic."

"How did you know she was a fraud?" asked Mrs West.

"Several reasons," he said as he walked around the room, "Firstly I heard reports from a source of a fraudsters in the area. It didn't take much time to track down our Madam Kline. All I needed was a convincing disguise which was helped in no small part by my secretary Jane here" - she gave a sheepish wave - "Who here noticed the broken doorbell?" everyone put their hand in the air. "Of course you did. Just as it was intended. Reset by the young boy after each person entered to make you feel uneasy. Just as the freshly washed door hinges, now free of the lubricating oil produced such a lovely creaking. The area immediately around the hinges was the only clean spot in the corridor. An easy mistake," he taunted Anna, her expression starting to show the tightness of rage.

"But how did she know about Jennifer?" asked Mrs West.

"Obituaries my dear. That and a little research into each of you before you arrived," he explained.

"What about the knocking?" asked another voice from the group, "I saw with my own eyes there was nothing under the table."

"Would you care to take another look?" Eric lifted the edge of the tablecloth. At Anna's feet, wrapped in black cloth with only a face showing, was a young girl. She looked scared and clung to Anna's leg. The crowd gasped. "Your daughter I presume. And the grubby little boy. Your son. No doubt in the next room and at the other end of the tube in the ceiling there making phantom laughter" - he pointed out the hole in the ceiling with a small copper pipe sticking through - "Is he looking after the baby as well? How did you keep the baby quiet? Rum? Brandy?" he continued to circle the room knocking over cheap paper-mache props and what he could now see were painted book spines on old crates. Everything in the room was designed to deceive.

"Gin if you must know," Anna spoke for the first time in her actual voice; a broad north London accent, "I know exactly who you are Mr White. A preening prick who thinks he's better than the rest of us."

"And there you have it ladies and gentlemen. The true face of a con woman." The crowd started the grumble and leave in outrage. One woman spat at Anna as she left. Eric stood triumphant across the table from her, "You're finished Mrs Clune. I'll send you a copy of the article when its published. My treat." Anna pulled a knife from under her chair and pointed it at the door.

"If you know what's good for you you'll leave, now," she said through gritted teeth.

"Oh I'm gone already. See you in the news." He turned on his heels and left. When she heard the front door close she fell back into her chair exhausted and shaking.

"Mummy. Are you alright?" said the girl taking off the black cloth covering.

"I'm fine Gertie." She dropped the knife with a clang at her side and scooped her daughter up into a hug. She heard the baby cry from the next room. Disturbed by the racket no doubt. "Go help Harry settle Alfred back to sleep, I'll be along in a bit to tuck you both in." Once the kids had been dealt with, she sat in the dim light of the now defunct seance room and wept.

Five days was all it took for the article to be seen across London and Anna's business to be a talking point for all. A rapping at the door broke her gin haze. She opened the door and looked up bleary eyed into a familiar face under a police helmet.

"Ello Charlie, what brings you round here?" The brick outhouse in a uniform that was Charlie Spake stepped aside to reveal both Harry and Gertie looking at their feet. "What have they done now?" Anna sighed.

"We didn't do nothing mum, honest!" cried Harry. Charlie gave him a short sharp slap on the back of the head.

"Lying to your mum too eh? What would your old dad say?" he turned his face back to Anna, "Pickpocketing. Or trying it anyway. Their mark caught them in the act and when they ran off they nearly caused a carriage to overturn." Anna blushed.

"Get inside now. No dinner, go straight to bed," she told them through gritted teeth. They looked back at her sheepishly and tried to scoot past her knowing what would happen. She was too quick though, even with a drink in her, and gave each a spank on the backside as they came in. Harry jumped up and down clutching his bottom and sucking air through his teeth. Gertie cried. "I mean it. Bed!" she pointed at the door. Once they had left she turned back to the officer. "Want a drink Charlie?" she held up the bottle that set had down when she answered the door.

"I'd love to Anna but I'm on duty." He puffed out his chest and stood straight as an arrow. Then he cracked into a smile and winked at her, "Course I will." They settled in the living room. Charlie set his helmet on a box next to his seat and looked around at the boxes of seance props that surrounded them. "Things not going well then I take it?" He took the earthenware mug of gin she handed him. She slumped in her usual chair and took a big swig of her own drink.

"Rock bottom Charlie. Actually scratch that, I'm buried below rock bottom," She leant forward to clink her mug against his and slumped back again, "And now I cant even control the kids. They'll end up just like their dad, in a cell. Even this one." She put her hand in a box next to her seat and Charlie noticed the baby among the blankets.

"He's quiet," Charlie said with a knowing raised eyebrow. Anna lifted the bottle of gin.

"I had help. God knows its the only help I'll ever get. I just wish sometimes that things would be easier. You know? But how am I supposed to get out there and earn when I have to look after the kids?" She had spilled gin down her knuckles gesturing and now licked them clean.

"You need to talk to Tom. He set you up with the seance thing in the first place. I'm sure he'll have another idea. He may be behind bars but he's still your husband. He's probably working on a plan right now." He tapped the side of his nose and pointed at her.

"I doubt it. I ain't told him what's happened, and I don't intend to neither. Don't you dare say a word to him." She levelled her gaze at him. He held his hands up in mock surrender.

"Hey now, he may have kept me and the boys sweet over the years, but I don't owe him anything. I only promised to look in on you. I didn't say anything about spying on you. He can find out in his own time. But you know he will, eventually. He'll find the article sooner or later."

"By then I'll have everything sorted."

"Well as long as you're sure. You know where I am if you need anything." He drained his mug and stood up, placing the domed helmet back on his head and tipping the brim at her. She followed him to the hall as he opened the front door. "Hullo there," He bent and picked something up, "I didn't hear anyone knock did you?" he turned back to her with a small brown wrapped parcel in his hand. He flipped over the tag that was tied to the top. "It just says 'Anna'. Nothing else." He handed it too her and she ripped through the paper to find a square leather bound book of the deepest green.

"Probably something for Tom that needs fencing. I still get the odd stolen bits and pieces to pawn. I'll deal with it later" she put it on the side table in the hall and said her farewells to Charlie as he left. The click of the door sealed her again into the silence of her damp basement home. "Shut up!" she shouted at the kids as she passed their door and kicked it to silence their murmuring. "Anymore out of you tonight and I'll send you to the workhouse and be done with you." Silence followed and she nodded in admiration of her own mothering skills. Of course she did really love her kids, deep down. She just had a hard time showing it through the resentment she felt at having to deal with them all alone. She couldn't even ask Dotty upstairs to help anymore since her own daughter was taken to Bedlam. No, she had to handle it herself. At least when they were part of the seance con she could keep them in check. She went back to her dim room picking up the book on the way. she hoped that more gin would make a restful night's sleep but in the meantime she'd inspect the new piece of junk she had to sell on. She opened the front cover with a creak of leather that drew her attention fully. Maybe it was older than she'd thought at first. Pulling a candle closer on the table beside her for a better look, she tried to read the front page. Either she was already too far gone with the drink, or it was a language she didn't know. She closed the book again and inspected the cover. No marking on the front or the back. Just deep green leather that looked new but felt old under her fingers. She opened the tome again and flicked through several pages at the front. There were a mixture of writings in a strange language and symbols she couldn't quite focus on. In the margins and between lines she could see tiny handwriting. Too small for her to know whether it was even in English. From the rest of the text, she expected it wasn't and the gin vision wasn't helping. She flicked through. There appeared to be more pages in there than could reasonably fit between the covers. Many of them didn't match, giving the whole tome the feeling of a collection of pages from different books all stitched together. She realised that while most of the pages were paper, there were different thicknesses and textures. Some of the pages were even parchment, while one, she was sure, was papyrus. She started to recognise symbols further into the book. Tom had given her some books on the occult he'd stolen from a bookseller years ago. She'd used them to make props and learn metaphysical sounding words for the seances. This wasn't like any of the others Tom had given her though, and now as she flicked further there were words she could read. Archaic but she could read it. One page read, 'If to becometh ye wolven ist thou desire, then under a swollen goddess drive a blade of silver unto the stump of fresh felled oak. Jump ye over with feet over head and land there as a beast...'. This was accompanied by a crude illustration of a man performing a somersault over a tree stump. The margins of the page filled with more tiny writing. She flipped through more pages as she sipped her gin. The room was growing dim around her as the candle burned lower and the darkness crept in from the corners of the room. She stopped at a page and snorted in amusement. It read 'Mothers' help'.

"Well I definitely need that,"she said to Alfred as he stirred gently in the box next to her. What followed was a description that sounded more like an advertisement in The Lady than a page in an occult text. She read the page out loud. "If a mother in need you be, strike a match to candles three." Without even thinking she got up and was rooting around in a box for some candles. She found three black candles in a box of props. She arranged them on the table and lit them. She'd read enough rubbish about the occult to know it wasn't real, but something about the theatrics excited her. Besides, what was the worst that could happen? Even with the knowledge that nothing would happen, she was desperate enough to try. She read on. "Fix in mind your heart's desire as ye stare into the fire." She sat and thought. She wanted Eric White dead for what he'd done to her. No, that wasn't right. She wanted to be a famous medium. Famous for more than just being a fraud. She wanted everyone to know her. She wanted her name on everyone's lips. She looked at the open page in front of her and read the next part. "A mother's work is never done, recite the words the spell begun. Recite it twice to strike a deal, recital thrice will make the seal." The following short verse was hard to make out, but she gave it her best. "Whel Dinker Avage Tassa Lirach Ana Panzefur Aloren Laris." One of the candles extinguished itself leaving a trail of smoke curling in the air. She could hear the wind outside. She swallowed hard. Then for a second time. "Whel Dinker Avage Tassa Lirach Ana Panzefur Aloren Laris." Another candle followed the first. The darkness crept in further, and wind picked up outside. Anna could hear the howling of gusts against the house mixed with the sound of her thumping heart. She could stop right now. She should stop. She read again. "Whel Dinker Avage Tassa Lirach Ana Panzefur Aloren Laris." For a heartbeat nothing happened. She sat there staring wide-eyed at the remaining candle and holding her breath. then all at once a final mighty gust hit the house, then the wind stopped dead outside and the candle was snuffled out. The room was plunged into darkness and dead silence. Anna sat there for a moment dumbfounded; wide-eyed in the blackness and unable to move. A clicking creaking sound somewhere in the darkness of the room sent an electric tingle up her spine. She jumped up fumbling for the matches in her apron pocket and struck one.

"It's not polite to leave invited guests in the dark," an unearthly voice came from behind her. She jumped around with a gasp causing the match to go out as she did. "Tsk. Light a candle," the voice said in annoyance. Anna fumbled again, spilling matches all over the floor but somehow managing to keep hold of one. She struck it and saw the glint of eyes from the darkness in the corner of the room. She lit a candle and held it up to cast light at her visitor.

"Who are you?" she said, with a voice that betrayed all the fear she felt. Standing in the corner was a stern looking older woman. She stood, as if to attention, with her hands clasped over the worn handle of a slender blackthorn cane. Only her eyes moved, following Anna as she lit more candles around the room.

"Who am I? Shouldn't you know that? You did invite me after all," the unearthly voice was gone. In its place the harsh clipped voice of a woman of breeding. She sighed as she stepped forward, the floor length skirt of her dress sweeping the floor as she moved. "I am Governess Panzefur. You asked for help and I am here."

"Where did you come from?" Anna said straightening up the chairs and finding herself inexplicably welcoming this strange woman into her home. The governess lowered her head and levelled a cold stare at Anna.

"Best you don't ask," She swept over and sat in the seat opposite Anna's, "Thank you." Anna sat in her own seat. "Take a drink. It will calm your nerves." Anna didn't need telling twice. She poured herself a drink while keeping her eyes on this strange governess. She had the lines of age around her mouth and eyes, but it looked like they had been smoothed out. No not smoothed out, painted on maybe. Her hair was pulled tightly up and into a bun which had streaks of grey. The lace around her high collar and wrists of her sleeves was immaculate and white. She was pale skinned but not from powder as Anna had first thought. There was an air of hardness about her look. As Anna studied the small round yellow lensed glasses she was wearing she had the sudden realisation that the governess had yet to blink.

"You're not of this world." Anna said matter of factually.

"Correct. But I have certain influences that come in useful on occasion."

"Meaning?" asked Anna. The governess smiled showing a mouth full of teeth that were far too small and far too many.

"You have a want to be famous. To escape this life and go down in history. I have a want to take care of children. To educate them. You have the children," she looked at Alfred in the box and back to Anna, "I have the means to give you what you desire." She stroked a broach at her neck as she spoke. An insect of some kind trapped in purple glass. "Besides, the wheels have already been set in motion. Tomorrow I will begin the children's education.

You will need to prepare for your performance." She gestured around at the boxes of seance props. "I will provide the special guest that cements your place in history." Anna's excitement rose as she listened to the words of this creature she had surely summoned from thin air. She didn't care where she was from. She could give her what she wanted and take the kids off her hands too. To Anna, this strange lady was her fairy godmother. She dropped onto her knees in front of the governess.

"Thank you, thank you. Thank you a thousand times. How can I ever repay you?"

"You already have," she said as she stood, "I will call again at dawn." She stepped past Anna and into a dark corner. Anna stood and followed into the blackness with a candle. The corner was empty.

Daylight had barely grazed the damp cobbles of the street outside when three loud knocks came at the front door. Anna awoke in the chair she had fallen asleep in and straightened out the knots in her back and neck, regretting her sleeping position. She was used to the hangover and so she made her way easily to the front door through half lidded eyes with a baby on her hip. The knocks came again. Louder.

"I'm coming, I'm coming. Keep your blooming hair on," she called back. She flung open the door to an early morning chill and the stern looking governess Panzefur.

"Please be more prompt in future. I did say dawn after all." She swept passed Anna in a glide and let herself into the children's room. Anna rubbed her eyes and tried to keep up with the lady she thought she'd dreamt. The reality of last night came crashing in as the governess struck the floor three times with her slender gnarled cane. "Wake up this instant," She ordered. Gertie awoke immediately and stared like a frightened puppy at the figure in the room. Harry stirred in his sleep.

"Go away. I'm not done sleeping," He tried to say whilst yawning. The governess moved to him in quickly and slickly as Gertie scurried away.

"Get up now or I will not be responsible for my actions." She flung the threadbare sheet off the boy and grabbed his wrist. He opened his eyes in shock and locked eyes with the creature holding him. He jumped out of bed looking around the room. Gertie was in one corner looking just as scared as he felt. His mother was in the doorway looking in with red eyes as she wrestled with a now very awake Alfred. The governess straightened herself up and stepped back.

"Gertie, Harry, this is governess Panzefur." Anna explained and she stepped gingerly into the room to stand beside the stern statue of the governess. She's going to be looking after you while I sort out a few things. Get us back on track. You can call her...?"

"You will not call me," finished the governess, "Your mother will address me as governess or Panzefur. You will remain silent unless asked to speak. Do I make myself clear?" She turned her head to look at the scared children and cocked her thin eyebrow.. "I said do I make myself clear?" she barked. The children nodded. "If you have a question then you may raise your hand and wait to be invited to speak. You may reply yes Pan or no Pan and always remember your pleases and thank yous. Do I make myself clear?" They didn't answer. She raised her cane and lowered it quickly onto the floor creating a bang that seemed far to loud and making everyone jump.

"Yes Yes, we understand," said Harry as he looked at Gertie who was nodding away frantically.

"Obviously you do not!" replied the governess as she lowered her face to Harry's, "Yes, What?"

"Yes Pan," he said lowering his gaze.

"Excellent, it appears you can be taught. Get dressed and meet me outside in five minutes. Do I make myself clear?"

"Aren't you going to help us get dressed mummy?" asked Gertie.

"No she most certainly will not. Your mother is very busy and should not be standing idly around when there is work to be done in the other room." The withering stare she gave Anna was all that was needed for Anna to hand over the baby and dash to the next room to start work preparing for her return to seances. "And don't even think about asking me, I am your governess, not your nanny. You will learn to fend for yourself in this cruel world or die trying." Gertie looked as if she would burst into tears at any moment. "Four and a half minutes." She announced as she settled baby Alfred and left them to get ready.

A few minutes later and the two children left their mother who was in a whirl of action in the living room, boxes being unpacked and items flung about everywhere. They headed out into the crisp morning. Standing at the top of the steps waiting for them was governess Panzerfur holding onto the handle of an ornate baby pram neither of them recognised. It was black and shiny with a scalloped hood that covered Alfred's face as he lay snuggled among soft grey blankets, fast asleep.

"Gertie you look a frightful mess. Did you dress all by yourself?" Panzefur asked with that raised eyebrow.

"Yes Pan," she answered trying to straighten her skirt.

"Then that's all that matters. Tomorrow you will do better. Yes?" her voice had softened.

"Yes Pan," said Gertie, happy that she wasn't being told off as she'd thought she might be and feeling a little less scared of this lady in light of the morning.

"Maybe tomorrow you'll grow wings and fly too," said Harry, laughing at his sister who he had refused to help get ready. His amusement was short lived though as quick as a flash Panzefur lashed out a hand and slapped the back of his neck.

"Your life could depend on your sister one day. Remember that. Now come along, I have an old friend I need to call in on and we have a walk ahead of us. Fall in line and keep up." At that she started down the road at a brisk pace. Harry followed close behind, holding his neck, and Gertie brought up the rear, occasionally having to jog a little to keep up.

They walked without breaking stride. It appeared luck was on their side as every time they came to a road or a crossing it was clear for them to proceed. Gertie had her hand up to ask how long it was going to be but being at the back she went ignored. Soon enough the unmistakable smell of the Thames came into their nostrils; the mixture of rot and decay under the rushing, slightly salty water. They passed by fish stalls where entrails had been left in the gutter for cats and rats to feast on before they got washed away. Then they were descending a slope down to the water itself. The tide was out, and at this point there was a stretch of shingled bank they could walk on. The Pram got caught in the gravel but Panzefur just pushed through without seeming to use any effort. Gertie hopped along the tops of rocks to avoid walking on the gravel that sent Harry skidding and sliding along as they both tried to keep up.

"Eli!" called Panzefur in a voice that cut through the chatter of the dozen or so people searching the bank. Ahead of them one of the men stood straight and with a glint of fear in his eyes.

"Panzy?" He called back in a gruff voice. Then looking closer and confirming it was her he rushed over, snatching the flat cap from his head and ducking low to her in an almost courtly bow. "It really is you. Long time no see. What brings you here? And with kiddies too." What was that look Harry caught in this Eli's eyes, whoever he was. Greed? Hunger?

"You still talk too much Eli. Didn't I teach you anything?"

"I'm sorry. Yes Pan," he said bowing his head. Then, like a child, he raised his hand.

"Yes Eli, you have a question?" she said.

"May I still call you Panzy?" he asked sheepishly.

"You may."

"Then begging your pardon Panzy, but what brings you down among the mudlarks and bone-grubbers?"

"What's are mudlarks and bone-grubbers?" asked Harry and earning another slap on the neck for not raising his hand. Eli flinched at the contact. He looked at Panzefur who nodded her agreement at his answering the boy.

"We is Mudlarks," he said, scratching his head and sticking his chin out to the group of dishevelled people on the bank, "Well at least they is. They skim through the shit and rubbish down here for lost coins and shiny things. I don't go in for none of that though, I goes for the bones." He opened his jacket to show them a collection of bones of all sizes. "Most of these is even animal today."

"Eurgh!" exclaimed Gertie pulling a disgusted face and sticking out her tongue.

"Now now," said Panzefur as she turned to the children. "Everyday you wash your bodies with soap," she sniffed the air in their direction, "Well maybe some days." She raised that eyebrow at them again. "One of the ingredients in your soap is bones. So you see without Eli and those like him, you'd stink even more than you do right now. So say thank you Eli, and in future think before you speak. Even the dirtiest jobs are there for a reason."

"Thank you Eli," said Harry and Gertie as they looked at their feet in embarrassment. Eli straightened in pride at having his job described in such glowing terms. But then Panzy always had a different way of looking at things.

"Eli," she said turning back to him, "I need the storybook. Have you kept it safe?"

"Of course," he said with a knowing wink, "When do you need it?"

"This evening, bring it to this address," she handed him a small slip of paper. "You do remember how to read?". He nodded at her and took the slip. Then she lent in and whispered something into his ear. Eli locked eyes with

Harry again with that look that made Harry feel uneasy, "I trust I make myself clear?"

"Crystal," said Eli.

"Excellent," She said, turning to leave, "Oh and be a dear. Tell Hammy I'm in town." With that she started walking off pushing the still sleeping Alfred in the pram. Harry and Gertie quickly caught up and, without having the chance to say goodbye to Eli, they were soon back on the slope and heading away from the river.

They walked at a much more reasonable pace now. The strange governess pushed the sleeping baby with the 2 children following behind. Occasionally, the odd woman would slow down to rock the pram gently and make cooing noises into the open top of it whilst smiling that too many toothed smile of hers. It was approaching midday and the children looked exhausted as they walked. Panzefur took a sharp turn and the children nearly walked straight past the entrance to the park. They caught up soon enough and Panzefur lead them all to a quiet and shaded area beside a small pond with ducks. From under the body of the pram, she produced a basket and took out a blanket. She handed it to Harry.

"Lay that out on the ground" - he did as he was told - "Now take a seat you two. It's time for lunch. Your brother needs to be fed and changed too. So sit nicely and watch the ducks. I have sandwiches for you." The two children sat patiently on the blanket, listening to rumbling tummies and Panzefur took two paper-wrapped sandwiches from the same basket the blanket had been pulled from. They each unwrapped a parcel and found a slab of old cheese between two slices of slightly stale bread.

"Eurgh! This smells bad. We cant eat this!" said Harry, pinching his nose and holding the offending food away from him.

"You will because I said you will. Its good for you. Trust me," said Panzefur as she picked baby Alfred out of the pram.

"But its all mouldy!" complained Harry.

"Mouldy is it? There are always worse things to eat. Trust me." Panzefur clicked her fingers and a bloom of green mould patches spread across the top of both sandwiches right in front of the children's eyes. "See?" Gertie looked between the slices and found the cheese had been replaced with foul smelling fish and slimy tomatoes. She wretched a little. "Now I have told you it's good for you. So eat." Terrified, Gertie closed her eyes and took a bite without a second thought. It was bad, but not as bad as she had imagined. She still had a hard time keeping it down.

"I will not!" said Harry defiantly. He put the sandwich in his lap, crossed his arms and looked indignantly away. Gertie's whimper made him turn back to find Panzefur crouched in front of him, her nose almost touching his, her beady eyes burning through the yellow tinted glasses and into his very core. He scrambled back from her. She stayed motionless, baby Alfred happy in her arms, and she stayed crouched and followed the boy with her eyes. She slowly stood.

"There's are always worse things to eat," She repeated as she waved a hand over the discarded sandwich on the blanket. Her eyes never left Harry as the bread erupted into more mould blooms of yellow and brown. "Now eat it," she said calmly as she turned her attention back to the baby giggling contentedly in her arms. Harry crawled cautiously forwards. Gertie continued eating her lunch which was becoming more palatable as she continued. Harry peeled back a slice of bread to peer inside. The fish had been replaced with something unidentifiable. It was mushy and grey and slick with oil. Under that were several overcooked and squashed brussels sprouts. He lifted the mess to his face and gagged at the smells. Holding his nose he took a bite. It was bad. Not as bad as he had imagined, but still not pleasant. Whilst Gertie's lunch became less and less foul as she ate, Harry's remained much the same right to the last bite. They both felt a little queasy after, which was not helped by being in such close vicinity to Panzefur changing Alfred's bottom. Once he was powdered and dry and the sandwiches eaten, Panzefur sat down with them on the blanket. "Well done children. Here is a little treat for you." She took three small glass bottles from the basket and handed one each to them. The third she removed the cork from and plugged the top with a silver tubed attached to a rubber nipple. Gertie put her hand in the air. "Yes?"

"What is it?" she had removed the top and was peering at the yellowish bile substance inside.

"It is a treat. That is all. I promise you will enjoy it. Think of it as the reward for eating your lunch and doing as you were told." Whatever it was Alfred didn't mind as he sucked away at the bottle and giggled. Gertie and Harry both took a sip.

"It tastes like strawberries! My favourite," said a giddy Gertie.

"Mine tastes like toffee!" chimed in Harry.

"I will never steer you wrong children. All I ask is that you do as you are told. In return I can give you treats and presents." Exhausted from all the walking, they sat a while in the shade of the trees and watched the ducks swimming.

When Panzefur gently shook the children awake it was starting to get dark. They had fallen asleep on the blanket.

"Come along now children. It's getting late and I have something to show you on the way home." They stood and stretched and helped their governess fold the blanket. She put it into the basket and, after stowing that under the pram, they left the park. Evening was truly setting in as they walked along the cobbled roads. Darkness was spreading along the streets as the lamplighters set to work. On a particularly affluent road that neither of the children knew, Panzefur stopped. She slowly turned her head to look across the street. "Do you see that building there children? Do you know what it is?" she nodded towards a tall white stone building with an impressive staircase and pillars. At the top of the stairs stood huge double doors of dark wood. It opened occasionally spilling golden light into the street as people left the building.

"Is it a bank?" asked Harry.

"Very good," she said encouragingly, "In just a moment a man is going to leave the bank. His name is Mr Jameson. We are going to follow him home and I want you to watch him very carefully. Understand?" They both nodded their heads. "Good. Here he comes." The doors swung open for just a moment, the light obscuring the figure. When they closed they could all see the short dumpy man in a black pinstriped suit and bowler hat with an umbrella tucked under his arm. He took a deep breath in of evening air and smiled contentedly as he tipped his hat and said good evening to the people he passed. Panzefur and the children followed him on the other side of the street. The children tried hard to keep him in sight as they walked. Panzefur's eyes never left the man as she effortlessly navigated the pavement. Even Alfred was silent in their pursuit.

"Evening Simon" Mr Jameson waved to a newsagent sweeping the stoop of his shop.

"Evening Simon!" called back the newsagent. The friendly joke was comfortable between the two men who shared a name.

"How's business these days? Still keeping the financial world ticking over?" Simon the newsagent finished up the last bit of sweeping by sending a plume of dust away from his shop front and into the street with a flick of the broom.

"Oh you know how it goes. Never a dull day." Simon the banker pulled a coin from his waistcoat pocket to give to Simon the newsagent who had retrieved a broadsheet and folded it several times for the other Simon to tuck under his arm. "See you tomorrow. Good evening." He tipped his bowler to the newsagent who tipped his own flat cap back in response.

The children and Panzefur continued to follow the dumpy man and watched as he made several more similar stops. He made light hearted conversation, first with a pie seller where he picked up a greasy wrapped parcel, then a flower stall where he stopped to smell a bunch of roses and bought one to put into his button hole. He even stopped for several minutes to talk to another well dressed gentleman walking a small yapping dog. The dog spotted Panzefur and barked at her from across the street. The owner and Simon Jameson didn't notice the small dog cower and retreat to the safety of its owners side when Panzefur growled back in a low rumble. A few minute's walking later and they all watched as Simon Jameson climbed the steps to the front door of his red-bricked town house and let himself in.

"Well now children. What did you learn about Mr Jameson?" Panzefur turned to face the children, one hand on the pram and the other clutching the top of her gnarled cane. Gertie put up her hand, "Yes?"

"His first name is Simon."

"Well yes of course. Any idiot on the street could have learned that. What else?" Harry put his hand up, "Yes?"

"He works in a bank," Harry started listing on his fingers, "He can read. He's fat because he eats pies. He's friendly and happy. He has money and he likes flowers." Panzefur nodded her head slightly to one side with a look of appreciation on her hard face.

"Not bad. A little rudimentary, but on the face of it those would appear to be accurate observations. Well done boy." Gertie put her hand sheepishly into the air and looked at her feet, "Yes. girl. What is it?"

"Pardon me Pan but I don't think he is happy at all."

"And what prey tell gave you that impression?"

"His eyes. He had sad eyes." Gertie chanced a look up then looked back at her feet. Panzefur knelt and lifted the girl's face with a thin cold finger and stared into her eyes. She smiled at the girl showing a row of small crowded teeth.

"Well done girl." She stood and started walking away pushing the pram. "Follow." She called over her shoulder. They did. They crossed the road to be on the same side as Mr Jameson's house. Several houses along and between two buildings they followed their Governess down an alleyway. A moment later and they were following her in to the garden of a house; Mr Jameson's garden. From here, they could see that one of the first floor windows was illuminated by lamplight inside. She pushed the pram to the side of building and leaned in to talk to the baby. "Hush for a little while my sweet one and sleep." She walked to stand beneath the window which was several meters above her. "Come children. Stand with me and face the wall." They both did as they were told. Gertie shivered a little in the chill of the evening. "Now, you must be very quiet. Small voices only. Understand?" She looked to each and seeing them nod in acceptance the tapped the floor lightly with her cane. At the soft thud of wood, the mound of turf lifted all three in the air; raised by unseen and unfelt hands. Both children gasped as they slowly floated up to peer into the window of Simon the banker.

Gone was the jolly, chubby man they had followed on the street. Here sat a pitiful lump already three glasses deep into a bottle of whiskey: slumped on the edge of a well worn armchair; hair tussled; shoes and waistcoat discarded to the corner of the room. He wept into his lap as he tore open the top buttons of his shirt and drained his glass. His shaking hand poured another large measure from the rapidly depleting bottle. He took another sip then sat in the dim light alone, weeping and thinking.

"I said he was sad. Didn't I say that Pan!?" Gertie excitedly whispered.

"Yes you did child," Panzefur whispered back, "You see people are only ever really themselves when they are behind their own walls and feel safe. Everything else is just a mask. On the street, you would never suspect that Mr Jameson here had lost a lot of money today. More than most people would earn in several life times. Some people have lots of masks." Panzefur said as she scratched at the side of her face unnoticed by the children. "Learn how to make those masks and people will never know if you're sad, angry or lying." Simon Jameson suddenly stood up and walked to another room.

"Where is he going Pan?" asked Harry.

"Just watch," she told him. A moment later and Simon stumbled back into the room holding a small polished mahogany box. He set it down on the table by his seat and lifted the lid. From their vantage point they could see several lines of tortoise shell set into blue velvet. Simon drained another glass of whiskey and sat next to the box looking at his feet. "His father was a gentleman barber," Panzefur explained to the children as Simon reached over without looking up. He took a single straight razor from the box and with a flick of the wrist exposed the shining blade to the lamp light. All at once he looked to the heavens and without a sound ran the blade across his throat. His vitality oozed and sprayed from the slash as his eyes bulged. He choked out a cough and slumped lifeless back into the chair. Both children looked up at Panzefur with ashen faces. Harry even had a tear in his eye. "It's simply the way of the world children. Wait here." She floated back from the side of the building into the surrounding darkness. Harry was straining his eyes to see her when Gertie tugged at his sleeve.

"Look," She whispered pointing at the room. Panzefur was inside. She took something from the box and left through the doorway, "Where did she go?"

"I'm right here," Panzefur's reply scared them both, but there she was, as if she hadn't left, "Here a gift each for being such good students." She held out her hands and on each upturned palm was an ornate tortoise shell handled straight razor. "Be careful with them. I will not be responsible for lost fingers." They each took one as they felt themselves float back down to the ground.

"Ello Pan," came a voice in the darkness by the pram. Eli stepped forward clutching something to his chest.

"You have it. Excellent," said Panzefur, taking the book he was holding so preciously, "Did you pass along my message?"

"Yes Pan," bowed Eli, "It wasn't easy. He's under guard at the moment."

"I expected nothing less from Hammy. Thank you Eli. I will call on you soon when I need you." He scraped the floor with his bow as he left into the darkness of the garden. "Come children. Let us get you home." Another hour walking in their new formation of Panzefur followed by Harry with Gertie bringing up the rear and they were back home and heading to bed. Anna had passed out through sheer exhaustion and so didn't notice the strange lady place the baby back in the box by her side as she slept. Governess Panzefur looked around the room. Anna had made a good start making the room into a suitable stage for her grand performance. She left them all sleeping in the dank darkness.

The next morning saw a bright and alert Anna awake before the crack of dawn. She felt invigorated and ready for the world. She was so ready that she had opened the front door to the knocking before the third knock even came. "Good morning," She greeted the Governess, "I trust the children were no bother yesterday."

"They were adequate, thank you," replied Panzefur as she swept past Anna and into the hall.

"I've nearly finished making the room ready. Would you like to come and see?"

"I have already seen. You're making progress but there is still much to do." Anna looked downhearted at the thought of more work. "Don't worry my dear. Small things really, trifles. But they most be done. No corner will be cut. It should take you no longer than a few hours. This afternoon you will make yourself presentable. Cut your hair, bathe and fix your clothes."

"Cut my hair? But I always wear a headscarf and the dirt and grime helps with the make up. You know, makes me look older." Anna pulled at her clothing looking uncomfortable and like a full grown version of Gertie. Panzefur flicked the tip of Anna's nose.

"Buck up girl. You are not Madam Kline, you are Anna

Clune. Remember that for that is who will be on show tomorrow."

"Tomorrow?" asked Anna with girlish glee, "Do you think I'll be ready?" Panzefur eyed the woman and sighed.

"Very well. Today the children will learn from home. I will set them tasks for the day and I will be on hand as your adviser. I will of course take care of the baby." Panzefur produced a silken purse from her skirts and rummaged inside. Anna noticed several thick black hairs sprouting from the purse. "Sow's ear," said the Governess in answer to Anna's obviously interest. "Transforming the mundane into the extraordinary is a gift. Ah! Here it is." She pulled a slim pocket journal from the purse and held it up. Gold letters across the front of the brown cover stated 'letters and numbers'. "I believe we have today's lessons for the children in hand."

It took less than twenty minutes for Panzefur to have the children awake and ready for the day. Each one was given a slate and slate pencil and told to dress and make a comfortable seat. When they were done she wheeled in a larger slate of her own.

"Wow! It's like a real classroom. Where did you get that?" asked Gertie in awe.

"No raised hand, no answers," she stared at Gertie who looked at her shoes again, "Your clothes are better today girl. Boy blow your nose, you have a snot bubble." Harry popped the bubble for mucus with his finger then wiped his sleeve across his face.

"Today we are staying home. Your mother and I are very busy and do not wish to be disturbed. Understood?"

"Yes Pan," they said in unison.

"Excellent. Copy down these words. And fill the board. When you are finished clean your board and start again. I will be back with new words soon." She turned the board to reveal immaculate script. Harry raised his hand. "Yes?"

"What is abo, abomni..."

"Abomination," she said for him, "An abomination is a disgusting thing and should be treated in a fitting way. Now. Carry on and I will be back shortly." She left them with the board to write out again and again 'My fellow man is an abomination.' Every so often she would come back and check on their work, telling Gertie how messy her handwriting was and praising Harry for his excellent writing. She would change the words written on the board each time then leave the children to copy such phrases as 'Greed is divine' or 'My body is a temple of flesh and bone'. By lunchtime she had started to include more obscure writing such as 'Ancients whisper in the darkness through cracks in the void' among the other sentences. They had just spent twenty five minutes writing and rewriting 'Innocence is delicious' when Pan came in with a grubby tray laid out with small pies and tarts. After the incident with the sandwiches the previous day, neither of them were brave enough to mention the patches of pastry that had started to turn white and fuzzy and so just ate without complaint. They were both pleasantly surprised with how good the lunch was. She came back to collect the tray with baby Alfred on her hip suckling away at one of those bottles of liquid. "Well now," she said with an almost warm smile, "That is what I call a lesson well learned. Here." She took two more bottles from somewhere among her skirts and tossed them one each,

"You've earned it." The children greedily unstopped the bottles and slurped down the yellowish liquid contentedly. She allowed them ten minutes respite before another sentence was left for them to copy and their lessons continued. Anna meanwhile had completed all of the decoration in the living room that governess Panzefur had not so subtly suggested. All the cheap looking home made props were taken away in place of the few real items she had. A crystal ball and several gems. Half a dozen books on the esoteric arts. A brass censer which held a sweet incense Panzefur had given her. The walls and floors had been washed. The large table was once again in the centre of the room and had been polished to a shine. The room looked positively Spartan, but undoubtedly the perfect stage for a seance. Anna spent the afternoon under the gaze of the governess sewing her best dress back to presentable condition and repairing seams and holes.

"Do I really need a full wash?" asked Anna as she flicked out her dress and inspected her handiwork in the light.

"Oh yes," said Panzefur as she bounced Alfred in her arms making him coo and giggle, "Everything has to be perfect. Trust me." She said peering over the rim of her glasses and grinning at Anna. "In fact I have a gift for you." She held out her hand and Anna took the offered item. A small smooth ivory coloured bar of soap. "A gift from a friend of mine."

"Oh my goodness," said Anna noticing the lack of natural light in the hallway outside, "What time is it? The children need dinner."

"I have already dealt with that." And she had. The

children had been treated to a dinner of boiled cabbage and turnip slop, which both recoiled at but ate without complaint. "You just see to yourself. Don't worry about washing just yet. I will take the children out tomorrow and give you time alone to prepare. We'll be back in time for the big show." She assured her.

"Thank you, thank you a thousand times," said Anna on her way out to find a bite to eat and leaving Panzefur alone with the children. Panzefur put Alfred in the box and told him to sleep, which he did. She took out the book that Eli had given her and went to the children. They both laid on their pallets of rags, exhausted from the day of mental exercise.

"Its nearly time to sleep children. But before you do, I have a very special bedtime story to share with you." She pulled up a chair and invited them to sit beside her on the floor. She opened the book on her lap and up popped the paper cut out of a shop front. Both children gasped.

"Its a pop-up book!" said Harry.

"Its a very special pop-up book," said Panzefur, stroking the page, "This is the story of a pretty young girl in a shop. Her name is Collette." Panzefur pulled a tab and the shop doors opened revealing the cut out of a girl.

"Why does she look so sad?" asked Gertie.

"She's sad because she has worked at this shop for a long time. You see there is another lady at the shop that Collete has to listen to and take orders from. Her name is Wilma." Panzefur turned the page and the a shop interior appeared in pop-up with two figures. The first sad girl and another older lady with a mean look on her face.

"Wilma doesn't like Collette because Collette is pretty and young, so she makes her do lots of dirty jobs." Panzefur flicked through several pages. Up popped Collette on one page sweeping a chimney, on another cleaning chamber pots. Each job dirtier than the last. Finally a very angry looking Collette popped up with folded arms. "She was very angry with Wilma and hated how she was treated. But Collette was also very smart, and she had a plan." Another tab pull turned Collette's expression from angry to devious. "This particular shop sold lots of very pretty things. Pretty and expensive." Turning the page revealed shiny pictures of earrings and necklaces studded with what the children thought must be real gemstones. "Collette would often hear Wilma telling people how she would buy some of these things if she could afford them. So one day when Wilma was busy and thought Collette was sweeping in the cellar, Collette stole a pretty bracelet and put it in Wilma's coat pocket." The page showed Collette holding a shining object over the coat. The tab made the arm go up and down putting the bracelet into the coat. The next page was mean old Wilma finding the empty spot and calling for police. "Wilma couldn't believe her eyes. 'Thief!' she shouted to attract the attention of a passing policeman." The tab raised the figure of a policeman who looked a lot like Charlie Spake, the policeman who told their mum what they'd done. "The policeman interviewed both Collette and Wilma while they waited for the shop owner to arrive. Collette was smart and told the policeman that she had been ordered into the basement by Wilma and wasn't surprised Wilma had noticed something was missing as she often said how much she would like it for herself. Therefore she was bound to notice the empty space. The shop owner arrived and told the two ladies to go home." The page showed an unhappy old man talking to the policeman while the ladies collected their things. "The policeman had his suspicions though thanks to the cleverness of Collette and he searched both the ladies before they left. Collette was clear" The pop up confirmed this. "But when the policeman searched Wilma he found the missing bracelet." The pop up showed a shocked Wilma being restrained by the policeman holding up the shiny bracelet. At the back of the shop stood a smiling Collette. "Wilma was found guilty of the crime and sent to prison." An unhappy Wilma popped up behind bars. "And Collette got the job she wanted and an assistant of her own." A happy Collette was sending a young girl into the chimney to sweep. Panzefur closed the book and looked at the children. "Proof if ever needed that if you want something, then you have to be smart and take it. Now off to sleep."

"That was a great story," said Gertie as she nestled in her rags and yawned.

"Good night Pan," said Harry.

"Good night children." She left them in darkness. Anna had returned whilst Panzefur was reading and so she took her leave of the family for the day.

Morning brought anxiety and apprehension for Anna. She awoke with the realisation that today would change her life forever. In all the hurry to get things ready, she had neglected to actually prepare what she was going say at the seance. She stopped chewing her lip when Panzefur walked into the room.

"Oh. I didn't hear... did you knock governess?" she looked puzzled at her strange saviour.

"I hardly think that is necessary now my dear," she replied with an amused smile playing on the corners of her thin mouth, "Is something the matter?" Panzefur swept over in a glide and sat opposite Anna as the damp dawn light spilled in from the hall.

"Well," she hesitated.

"Yes?"

"I'm just a little nervous I suppose. I don't really know what I'm supposed to do tonight." She wrung her hands together.

"You don't have to do a thing. I told you. I will take care of everything. It will come as naturally to you as breathing. Trust me. You will be a spectacle." Panzefur placed a cold hand over Anna's. "Now my dear. You just rest today. I will take the children out to give you some peace and when we return it will be show-time." She scooped baby Alfred out of the box of rags. "This one is getting heavy." She went to wake up the children who were already awake and getting dressed, "Good morning children."

"Good morning Pan," they said in unison.

"We heard you talking to mummy so I decided we should get ready," said Harry, pleased with himself.

"Initiative. I like it. Meet me outside in ten minutes." The children only needed five minutes to be on the street outside their basement dwelling and ready to go. Pan was waiting with Alfred in a pram and started walking as soon as the children joined them on the cobbles. She walked slower today allowing Harry and Gertie to walk either side of her. Gertie raised a hand. "Yes?" said Panzefur without looking at her.

"Where are we going today Pan?" she asked. Pan stopped and looked at her with that same hint of amusement playing on her lips.

"We're going to see a special friends" she told her. After a lot more walking they stopped across the road from an imposing sandstone building with a dome and spire set atop. "Children. Welcome to the Old Bailey courthouse."

"Wow." They were both in awe of the impressive structure.

"Is that were your friend lives?" asked Harry.

"He's more of a frequent visitor," replied Panzefur.

"You mean we get to go inside?" an excited Gertie asked.

"We will. First a quick stop. Come along, and don't make a sound. Understand?" They both nodded their acceptance and Panzefur lead them to the side of the building where a secluded alleyway sheltered two men in conversation. The older, distinguished looking man had his back to the wall and beads of sweat ran down his balding head. The younger, taller man had his hand pressed against the wall next to his companions head and was talking directly in to the older mans ear in a low voice. Panzefur and the children stood obscured by several boxes and watched as the older man suddenly turned very red in the face and pushed the younger man away.

"How dare you insinuate such a disgusting thing sir! Do

you have any idea who-" His sentence cut short with a yelp as the younger man grabbed him by the lapels and effortlessly lifted him gently off the ground. He brought the man's face close to his and said in a very clear and well spoken voice.

"I know exactly who you are. Better than most I'm guessing David, or should that be Daddy?" David was visibly trembling as the taller man put him down just as effortlessly as he had lifted him. He took something paper-like from his pocket and held it up for the now very pale David to see. Splaying the photographs like a deck of cards.

"Where did you..." he tried to grab the pictures and was rewarded with an iron grip around his wrist.

"Now now. I'll keep your little secret, if you keep mine. Deal?" David said nothing in response so more pressure was applied to his wrist. "Deal?" the younger man repeated as David groaned in pain.

"Yes yes, deal." He stumbled back onto his backside with the release of his arm.

"Excellent choice old boy." The young man rapped on the door a few paces from their encounter and it swung open. "After you," He gestured to the now recovered David. Before following him in to the building though, the younger man stood straight and sniffed the air. He turned to peer into the shadows where Panzefur and the children watched. For a moment there was silence. Then he sniffed a final time and went inside, letting the door swing closed behind him.

"What was that all about Pan?" asked Harry with a raised hand.

"A lesson children," she knelt to their eye level, "Remember, some of the most interesting and important things in life happen in the back alleys. Now, come along." She stood and pushed the pram back into the sunlight and proceeded to the main courthouse entrance with children in toe. The children sucked in breaths of appreciation at the interior of the place. They tried to take in all the details of the carvings in mahogany wood and the enormous oil paintings and busts and that lined the walls, but it was impossible whilst keeping up with Panzefur. She turned down one corridor after another until they were in a long wood panelled hall where a uniformed man guarded a door. She didn't break stride as she walked to the door reached passed the guard to take hold of the handle.

"Whoa whoa whoa!" said the man taking hold of Panzefur's arm, "You can't go in there. Closed session. Not for the public." She snapped her head around to look at him. Her body was deadly still as only her eyes moved and glared at this barrier before her. He let go and took a step back. "As you were miss," he said in a drone. He took his place back where he stood and ignored Panzefur as she turned the handle and led the children into the upper viewing area of the courtroom.

"Take a seat children and be quiet. No one will see us up here," she whispered to them. She put a finger to her lips and shushed Alfred who stopped gurgling and drifted straight off the sleep. They all took seats on the rough wooden benches and waited. They didn't have to wait very long before two men wearing red gowns and powdered white wigs entered sat at different desks facing the raised area at the front. A man was brought into the room by a guard and sat down in a small holding area to one side.

"That's the man from the alleyway!" said Gertie in an excited whisper. Panzefur shushed her.

"All rise," called a voice from somewhere beneath them, "For the honourable Judge David Skipper." The children and Panzefur did not stand as the few other people did. Out stepped Judge David Skipper in his red gown and large curly wig. His sense of authority turned him into a different man from the one they had seen outside. Gertie and Harry looked at each other with slack jaws then turned to Panzefur. She gave them a knowing nod and turned back to the courtroom.

"Thank you council for the time to deliberate," the judges voice resounded with practised ease in the room, "It is unusual for a case to be so vile, so malignant as to warrant a closed trial and to be kept from the public. Both sides have presented their cases for and against the accused which I have now had chance to fully assess. Whilst there is no denying that the defendant William Hamilton has been accused of behaving abhorrently in the past, in this case I find the evidence too muddied to place him at the scene of the crimes." David took a drink of water and patted sweat from his brow. William Hamilton simply smiled at the judge. "And so it is this court's decisions that the defendant be released immediately under a verdict of not guilty." He punctuated the verdict with a whack of the gavel. He stood to leave in haste before the grumbling prosecution lawyer could say anything. William Hamilton also stood, straightened his suit jacket and left through the same door he'd entered with his head held high. Both lawyers collected their papers and left. Their faces the pictures of comedy and tragedy. When the room was clear, Panzefur stood, collected the pram and left the courtroom with Harry and Gertie following. They stepped into the sunlight of the street to be greeted by a familiar voice.

"Hello Governess. Eli said you were back" William Hamilton was leaning against the wall of the courthouse puffing clouds of sweet smelling smoke from his pipe.

"Hello Hammy. You got outside quick." Both children looked at each other. So this was Hammy.

"I see you have some sweet looking children with you." He knelt down to both of them clutching his pipe between his teeth to grin at them, "What are your names little ones?"

"I'm Gertie," said Gertie.

"And I'm Harry. What did they think you did?" Harry wiped his nose with his sleeve.

"Well now, this ones manners still need a bit of work governess." He winked at Gertie conspiratorially, "Well Harry, since you asked so nicely. Several girls have been hacked to ribbons in the east end. Parts of them have been eaten by who ever did it." He leaned closer and closer to Harry's face. Harry gulped.

"Did you do it?" Harry asked trembling. Hammy stood up laughing loudly and wiping a tear away from his eye.

"Of course not. Goodness gracious. I'd never eat someone." He rustled Harry's hair and turned back to Panzefur, "Eli said you wanted to talk to me?"

"Yes. Children stay here." She picked up Alfred from

158

the pram and walked several paces away leaving the children to guard it. Hammy followed her. They talked in hushed voices that neither child could hear. Several times Hammy looked over to them and nodded or smiled.

"What do you think they're saying?" Gertie was pulling on Harry's sleeve. He pushed her off.

"Get off me. I don't know and you're no help pawing at me." Just then Hammy laughed loudly, nodding in agreement to something. He saluted the children with his pipe.

"Lovely meeting you both. Until next time." And he walked away.

"What a very strange man," Gertie said as Panzefur placed Alfred back into the pram.

"Orphans are sometimes a little odd," said Panzefur.

"He was an orphan? I thought all orphans grew up to be factory workers He looks like a businessman," Gertie said confused.

"I like to look after my children. I made sure he was well taken care of in the end." Panzefur finished tucking in the baby and started walking.

"I wish I was an orphan, then I wouldn't have to live with you," Harry pushed his sister hard enough that she fell and skinned her knee. She started crying.

"You're a bully Harry!" she cried. Panzefur stopped abruptly and in a flash was crouched in front of the crying girl. She put a hand over the cut knee and spoke in a very quiet voice.

"If you don't want to be bullied, don't be a victim. Now get up." She stood, releasing Gertie's knee as she did. The cut was gone. With Gertie being upset, Harry feeling guilty and Panzefur being Panzefur, they walked the rest of the way home in silence. Dark was closing in as they reached the top of Crabtree Lane. Anna was standing on the street, arms folded, looking this way and that. When her eyes found them walking up the road she jogged over to meet them.

"Where have you been?" Anna was a wreck of nerves, "Tonight's the night and I need you Governess. You hear that? *I* need you, not them." She pursed her lips and thrust her chin at her own children.

"Calm down dear. Go and boil a kettle while I settle the children for the night. I have something that will help. Well go on!" she barked at the hysterical woman. Anna dashed down the stairs and into their home to boil water. "Pay no mind to her children. Some people are meant for different things than being mothers. But that's why I'm here. Now go and get ready. Dinner will be in your room whilst I help your mother."

"Yes Pan," they both said and followed their mother into their home.

"What is it?" asked Anna taking a sip of the grey liquid Panzefur had made her after feeding the children.

"It will calm your nerves. Relax you. We don't want you to get too excited now do we." Panzefur was walking around the room and adjust the position of items as Anna sipped away at the bitter liquid. Anna's legs felt wobbly under her.

"Does this have gin in it? I feel a bit drunk"

"No dear, no gin. Just a little herbal recipe I picked up some time ago." Anna started to feel a little woozy and accidentally let the cup slip from her fingers.

"Oh no," She struggled to say, "The mess, I need... clean... seance..." she collapsed on the floor.

Candlelight hurt her eyes when she woke up. She tried to bring her hands to her face to massage her temples but her arms where fixed in place. Confused she tried to get up but she couldn't move her legs either. Confusion turned to panic as she looked up to see her hands had been tied. Her legs too she now realised. She had been clothed in the newly repaired dress and tied to the table with lengths of torn cloth. Another wad of fabric had been put in her mouth to gag her.

"Oh good. You're awake. I was starting to think you'd had too much of my special tea. A little nightshade goes a long way." Anna struggled against her restraints as Panzefur stepped from the darkness. "Shush shush my dear. Nothing to be done now but play out the game. I promised to make you famous and I have just the little helper to make that happen." Panzerfur swept her hand towards the door and it creaked open to reveal a tall man silhouetted against the lamp light of the corridor.

"You gagged her Pan. That's a shame. I like to hear them scream," said Hammy stepping into the room. Anna squirmed on the table and bucked around trying to free herself. It was no use. Hammy reached into his jacket pocket and pulled out a slender blade as long as his forearm with an ivory grip. "Any preferences?" he asked

"Just make it sensational my dear. You are the artist after all. I trust your judgement," Panzefur told him as she inspected her nails. Hammy breathed heavily though his grinning teeth and advanced on the terrified woman tied to the table. "Wait!" Panzefur held up a hand. She walked over to the box of blankets and picked up Alfred. "Lets not spoil the innocence with such a show. I'll be next door when you're finished Hammy. Have fun." Panzefur left the room. She closed the door and stood quietly in the hall for a moment listening to Hammy's joyful laughter and cackles as he hacked into Anna Clune. Now it was time to deal with the children. The door creaked as she entered.

"What's happening next door?" asked Harry

"Just giving your mother what she asked for. But I'm afraid things are going to have to change around here." Panzefur motioned for them to come closer as she knelt down. Something crashed next door startling them both. "Hammy has come to help you all. Once he's finished with your mother he'll take care of one of you. But which one will he take care of?" She grinned a wide tiny toothed grin.

"You mean he's going to do away with us?" said Harry, turning white. Gertie was wide eyed and looking around, "Then do Gertie. She's a girl, she don't matter much." He took a step back from Panzefur as she stood.

"Deary me Harry. You do have the wrong end of the stick don't you," she said shaking her head. The door creaked open behind her and in stepped Hammy cleaning blood off his hands with a silk handkerchief.

"Which ones coming me with me Pan?" he asked her, eyeing the two children.

"What do you mean?" Harry asked

"She means this you stupid bully." Gertie pulled her hand from her tattered skirts and flicked her wrist. The tortoise shell handle almost too big for her grip as she slashed cleanly across her brothers throat. He reminded her of a fish with those bulging eyes and soundless smacking lips. He dropped to the floor with a wet thud. "Is it time to go now?" She asked. Panzefur cradled the girl's face and looked deep into her eyes.

"I was hoping for a girl. So much more civilised," said Hammy, lighting his pipe.

"Well done," said Panzefur, "Hammy will look after you, just as he was looked after. One day it will be your turn." Gertie walked to Hammy and took his hand.

"I'm ready to go now," she told him.

"Good. The smell of poverty is making me nauseous." They left the dank air of that basement hovel for the last time. On the street, they were greeted by a familiar face.

"Good evening Panzy." Eli practically scraped the ground bowing.

"There is a job down there for you Eli. The boy in the front room. Plenty of lovely bones for you. Make it messy," she told him, "But don't go in the back room. Understand?"

"Yes Pan, of course," he said, scuttling away down the stairs and disappearing inside. Panzefur looked down at Gertie.

"Goodbye Gertie. Hammy will look after you from now on. It's time for me to leave. But I'll be back. One day." And she started walking away.

"Wait!" Gertie called out, "What about Alfred?" She pointed at the baby still in Panzefur's arms. Panzefur turned slowly back to Gertie. A wide grin on her face.

"Oh he's mine. Part of the deal." She bounced him in her arm a couple of times like a grocer weighing a cabbage, "Mm. So innocent." She turned away again.

"But-" Gertie was halted by Hammy gently pulling her back by the shoulder. She looked up at him.

"Its best not to think about it Gertie. Understand?" he said in a calming voice. She nodded up at him and turned back to catch a last glimpse of the Panzefur's skirt swishing into the darkness of an alleyway. "Come now," he took her by the hand, "Lets go home."

It took less than twenty four hours for the article to be all over London and spreading fast. Under the headline *Bethnal Bloodbath*, came this report.

"In a basement flat on Crabtree Lane, Bethnal green, a most horrific sight was discovered earlier this morn. The body of Mrs Anna Clune, a woman recently unmasked for fraudulent seances, was found brutally dismembered. An inside source at the police department described the state of the body as 'hauntingly beautiful'. It would appear that once the killer had butchered the body with the skill of a surgeon, he arranged the pieces in such a way as to give her the appearance of a grotesque angel. Another source went into more graphic detail describing the flayed lungs which had been removed and arranged like wings. One would be inclined to remember the similar case in Epping several years ago if not for the for the further discoveries in that basement of horrors. Mrs Clune had three children who were reduced to pure viscera which coated the floor and walls of the second room. The sight and smell making several experienced officers vomit profusely. Once a con artist and mother, she will undoubtedly be known forever after as the 'Bloodied Angel of Crabtree Lane'. - Eric White."

STORY FOUR

Appetite

Dear Ms. Richards.

I apologise in advance if you find the contents of this letter upsetting but I assure you it is something you will want to read. My name is Jerry and I sell Bibles. Not my real name, for reasons that will become abundantly clear, but it's as good as any other. You may remember me from a few weeks back. You very kindly offered me lemonade even though I could tell you weren't interested in what I was selling. That's okay, not many people are these days. But that's not why I'm writing to you, and I doubt you would find much help in a Bible anyway. No, I'm writing to tell you about a man named Tarrare.

Strange name right? Well it's an old French name for an old French man. He was born in 1772 to be precise. He was a very special man. A showman of the day. You see Tarrare had this unusual talent. He could eat vast amounts of food. More than his body weight in fact and all in a single sitting. Such huge amounts that his belly would distend and he would balloon up only to shrink back down again by the next day. He ate so much that his family threw him out because they couldn't feed him enough. So he did what any young man with a weird skill would do and joined a circus. There they would invite audience members to give him things to eat. Among the freaks he found a home and he could show just how strange his body was. People would give him whole bushels of apples and dozens of eggs. He would swallow them all down, but not before showing people just how big his mouth was. He could fit a whole dozen eggs in his cheeks. But he didn't just eat food. People would bring along corks from bottles, rocks, lumps of wood. He ate them all. Then there were the live animals. People brought along cats, rats and mice. Ripping open the bodies with his teeth, he would drink the blood then swallow them whole. Hours later he would regurgitate the skin and fur. People were horrified and delighted by the man that could eat anything.

Tarrare considered his ability a curse. His body would swell with all the food he ate, but the next day his skin would be loose and sagging. He was always hungry and could never find enough to eat. People were scared of his unusually wide mouth and extra teeth. After one performance in a small town in southern France, a group of thugs beat him up and stole what little money he had earned from his feats. Tarrare decided he'd had enough of people and wanted to get away from the circus crowds so he joined the army. After just three weeks on army rations he fell ill through malnourishment. The army doctors soon found out about his strange and wonderful body. In exchange for the rations of four soldiers a day, he allowed them to examine him. They found that as well as the extra teeth and amazing expanding and contracting stomach, he had a throat that could open up wide enough to swallow a whole cooked chicken. When a superior found out about this they decided to test his abilities as a spy. They sent him into enemy territory with a secret message in a wooden box which he swallowed with the intent to retrieve it later and deliver the message.

A medical curiosity he might be, but a spy he was not. He was almost immediately captured and put in prison. He held the message in the wooden box inside for more that thirty hours before he had to 'evacuate it'. But being so loyal to his superiors, he swallowed the box again. And again, and again. Eventually his captors posted a guard whose job was to sift through his leavings and find the box. The message was retrieved and his jailers let him go, laughing at the freak who carried a note which amounted to nothing more than 'If you receive this note we may use this man again'. Tarrare was humiliated and spent months roaming the country side of France eating what he could find from waste piles and tavern slop. He was the most malnourished he had ever been and looked like a skeleton wearing a very loose and sagging skin suit.

After collapsing in the street he was taken to a hospital where, as luck would have it, a discharged army doctor named Bison recognised Tarrare and took him into his care. They fed him huge amounts of raw meat and boiled eggs and within a month he was back to his old self but still complained of being hungry. Tarrare and Bison came to an agreement. He could live at the hospital if Bison could carry out his research on the man. Tarrare agreed and was given a room far away from other patients;

something the other patients were relieved about. You see, whilst he may have been odd looking, Tarrare also stank like a skunk who had been rotting for a month. The folds of his skin trapped all sorts of detritus which mixed with his profuse amounts of sweat to form the equivalent of a human cesspit. He produced vast amounts of foul gas from both ends and his breath stank worse than the rest of him. He spent several years in the hospital being treated with every known medication of the time. Nothing helped. He had been found eating discarded bandages from patients seeping wounds and hanging around the morgue. When a doctor's puppy went missing they found dog hair on his clothes. He denied it of course. Then a new born baby had been snatched from its mother in the night. Even though there was no proof, everyone suspected Tarrare and he was banished from the hospital.

From there, the history books are blank for several years. No one knows where Tarrare went until he turned up at another hospital. But I know. Tarrare did indeed eat the baby. He had been desperately hungry and whilst skulking around in the shadows looking for discarded items to eat he heard the baby crying. The mother, who was being treated with morphine, was unaware of anything as he crept into the room they occupied. Not even his stench woke her. The baby lay in the crib at the foot of the bed crying for its mother. Tarrare reached out to stroke its soft little head but the baby recoiled from him. He felt an anger he had never felt before at being rejected by something so new to the world. All the abuse he had suffered flooded his mind and in blind rage he snatched up the baby and stuffed it down his gullet; choking the squirming infant down like a fat chick in the nest with a juicy grub. Realising what he had done, he fled back to his room and hid till morning. It was only hours later that he was ejected from the hospital to fend for himself.

He walked for two days lamenting his actions but when sitting below a tree he realised something. Here he was, sat among a pile of fallen apples and he wasn't hungry. He had walked for two days and not eaten a thing, and he wasn't hungry. Had he been cured? He picked up an apple and bit into it. It was juicy and sweet. He had never stopped to taste things before, instead stuffing the food in. Half way through the apple he stopped, satisfied and not needing to eat any more. He jumped up and ran through the fields in elation, hopping and jumping between the trees. So taken was he with this mood that he didn't see the pond that he plunged into. Laughing he sat in the water and splashed around like a schoolboy. A young woman who had been washing clothes at the bank of the river came over to see if he was alright. She called from the bank and Tarrare instinctively turned his face away from her, not wanting to show his large mouth and ill fitting skin. But as he did so he caught his reflection in the water. The face that stared back had none of the strangeness he had come to know. He opened his jaws wide. The skin stretched to reveal the same wide mouth but when he closed it, the skin contracted back. He pulled at the skin of his body under his wet clothes. No sagging or loose skin. He could pull it out and stretch it just like his face, but it sprang back to something normal. The girl was still calling to him from the bank. He assured her he was fine and she smiled prettily at him. This young woman, Juliette, would become his wife by the year's end. She was the first person to show him true kindness and not recoil in fear. Rescuing him from the lake, she took him back to her father's farm where he started work as a labourer. The father was poorly so Tarrare did all of the heavy lifting. It was the wish of Juliet's father to see her married before he died and so, in a small church service, they became husband and wife. Juliette wore her departed mother's gold ring, and a few months later, after the passing of her father, she gave Tarrare her father's matching gold band.

Tarrare took to farm life and marriage with ease. When Juliette came to tell him she was pregnant he was scratching at the wedding band and the rash around his finger. He had caught the ring on a post the day before and it had cut his skin. Now the finger was swelling and skin around the ring sagged and oozed. After a week of the wound festering, he cut the ring from his finger. It took only a few hours for the wound to heal but the skin stayed sagging and loose from then on. He covered it with a glove to hide it from Juliette. Knowing the sentimental value of the ring he hammered it into a hair pin for his wife.

The baby was born in the spring, a daughter, followed less than a year later by a son. All this time Tarrare worked hard for his family and managed the farm well. It had now been three years since he and his wife had first met. He thought about the day he sat and was satisfied with half an apple as he now crouched behind the barn eating handfuls of threshed wheat stalks. The hunger was back on him. It had been growing for some time. He tried to hide his widening mouth with a scarf up to his nose and by wearing tight clothes to pull in the skin that had started to sag. Now though, he knew. He was cursed for life. But he also knew the cure. Babies go missing all the time in the country, he thought. Of course his wife would be distraught, for a while. But they could just ride out the grief together and have more children in the future. He was sure of it. So he decided to work till late that day and returned home under cover of darkness.

When he arrived home the house was all asleep. He crept to the bassinet that held his sleeping son and unwrapped the scarf from his drooling face. He stretched open his jaws and reached in to pick up his son. The growing light behind him made him turn around in shock to find a still very awake Juliette standing with a candle. She screamed at the terrible visage before her. The man she had loved transformed into this gape-mouthed horror. Motherhood instincts took over and to protect her children she snatched the golden hair pin from from her bun and lunged at the beast before her. She stabbed Tarrare several times before he clamped his teeth over her hand and bit it off at the wrist, swallowing the hand and pin in a gulp. The sharp golden point stabbed and pricked his gullet all the way down and embedding itself in his cavernous stomach. He screamed in pain as it made its way down and fled the farm leaving his family and any hope of a normal life behind.

This is where history picks up Tarrare again. He checked into a hospital complaining of the pain from the swallowed golden pin. The grotesque man of his past was now back in full and he lashed out in anger at those who tried to help him. Unable to retrieve the pin, Tarrare died.

So why, you might ask, am I telling you this? Tarrare thought that maybe he had done something bad as a child to earn his curse. But in reality the curse was not his. It had been passed down to him through his family. A rare and dirty little secret only a few knew about. The intense allergy to gold, the living flesh that kept the curse at bay. No one told him, or it had been forgotten. But these days you can find anything on the internet. Tarrare thought that he had to eat babies, but the truth is any human will do, as long as they are young and alive. When I saw your son at the park, I wanted to snatch him up right then and there, but I'm so glad I waited and followed him. Your daughter was so much sweeter. You may not have wanted a Bible, but at least it offered me the opportunity to disable the alarm. Of course she was much too big to swallow in a single meal, but once I got her home it was simple enough to remove her legs and arms but still keep her alive. She screamed for you as I swallowed her down. Of course nothing went to waste. I'm defrosting some leg for a snack as I write this letter. I hope this brings you some closure and you can stop posting missing posters around. Seeing her face gives me such bad indigestion.

Thanks for everything.

Jerry.

STORY FIVE

The Ghost Tour

Ian ran his fingers through his hair as he stood on the corner of the crossroads, waiting for his next group to arrive. Puffing out a plume of warm breath in to the chill of the evening, he looked at the sky. Heavy clouds threatened rain and he hoped that it wouldn't be the case. Flexing the brim of the top hat he held in his hands, he ran his fingers through his hair again and placed the hat on his head. He pulled a pocket watch from his long black coat. Almost time, he thought with relief. He enjoyed being the ghost tour guide most days, but standing here in the ring of light from the over head street lamp with the chance of a downpour was not one of those days.

"Hello?" a young man said, stepping into the light followed by a young woman and a young boy.

"Ah, hello and welcome. You're the first to arrive." Ian took a slip of yellowed paper from his pocket and unfolded it. "You must be Simon?" he peered over the top of his half moon glasses at the young man.

"That's right," he nodded.

"Which would make you Claire and this must be John."

He knelt down to the boy who clutched at his mum leg, "Hello young man. I'm Ian, pleased to meet you." John gingerly took hold of Ian's outstretched hand.

"Nice to meet you too." He said through the corner of his jacket, which he was chewing on nervously. Ian smiled and stood.

"Now mum and dad," Ian said for the benefit of John, "There might be some very scary parts on tonights tour. When I get to any particularly scary parts, I'll let you know in case we want to cover our ears." He winked at Claire.

"Isn't that a good idea." She squeezed her son's shoulder as two more people stepped into the light. Ian consulted his paper again.

"Good evening, you are?" He asked searching the short list of names. His eyesight wasn't what it was, even with the glasses.

"Um, I'm Julie, this is my wife Sam." Both leather clad women held up a greeting hand in unison.

"Nice to see I'm not the only one wearing all black." Ian straightened his coat, the short capelet flowing on the breeze.

"That's what happens when you marry a biker chick," said Sam. "You start to rock the biker chick fashion yourself," she giggled.

"I keep telling her it's not fashion, its more like armour, but she still insists on those flimsy little faux leather things." Julie told Ian.

"And I keep telling you I'm not wearing a dead cow. I can't be a vegan and wear skin. Besides, I only ride pillion and I have a gorgeous pink helmet thanks to you." She bopped Julie's nose with her finger.

"Vegans also don't eat bacon sarnies,"Julie said under her breath as she rolled her eyes. The look she received from Sam in response told her that she'd over shared in front of people and she'd be hearing about it later. Thankfully she was saved by a group of boisterous guys approaching them.

"Oi oi!" one of the three men called out.

"Gentlemen, welcome. If we wouldn't mind composing ourselves just a little, we do have children present." Ian said pointing at John who still clutched at his mothers leg.

"Sorry about that." One of them stepped forward with a little sway, "We've been celebrating our rugby team winning. Eight point lead." The two others cheered at this.

"That's great," said Ian in a hushed voice, "But let's keep it down just a little okay?" He winked at the three men who put their fingers on their lips.

"We'll behave. Sorry mate," one of the others said. Ian looked at his list.

"So you must be..."

"I'm John, this is Paul."

"And I'm Ringo," interrupted the third.

"That's Clive. He thinks he's funny," said Paul punching Clive in the arm.

"Another John. We'll have to call you Little John then won't we, like in Robin Hood," Ian said to the young boy who smiled at the thought of being named after a famous outlaw. Ian checked off the names, not happy at the thought of giving a tour to drunks. He hated drunk people, they always interrupted and made things messy. Then he heard it, the sounds of laughter and cackling. Oh no, he thought as five women stumbled into the light and joined the group. A hen party. Ian smiled through his anxiety, "Ladies! Glad you could join us. May I please point out that we have a child with us today and ask that you behave accordingly?"

"Oh look at the sweet little thing." A drunk woman wearing a penis whistle around her neck and a sash which read '#1 cock destroyer' knelt down to little John who was being swept behind his mother as she protected him from the loud drunk woman.

"Ahem!" Ian caught her attention and pointed at his own chest and neck indicating the inappropriateness of her accessories. She quickly stood and took them off, and blushing joined her group. "Thank you for joining us ladies." They all 'Wooed' very loudly. One of the women stepped forwards clutching her purse in her hands. She wore a grey skirt and brown cardigan with sensible shoes. All of which made the stripes of rainbow face-paint someone else had applied to her stand out by contrast.

"Hi," She waved meekly, "I'm Sharon, this is Kathy and-"

"Oh shut up and lighten up Sharon, jeez," said the woman that Sharon had pointed out to be Kathy. Kathy was dressed in nothing more than a white silky slip with fish net stocking, high heels, a veil. Several learner plates had also been sellotaped to her. "I'm Kathy, these are my girls, and I'M GETTING MARRIED!" She shouted followed by whoops from her entourage. Ian looked unimpressed at the outburst and raised his eyebrow at her. He said nothing. He simply stood and glared until Kathy, realising the world does not revolve around her, stepped back into the group.

Ian stared into the distance. His unfocused gaze and deep breathing made the surrounding group feel uneasy. They inched closer and looked at each other as the moment stretched uncomfortably on.

"Good evening ladies and gentlemen," Ian said in a booming theatrical voice making most of the group jump and giggle. His face was suddenly animated and looked from person to person with a practised eerie smile and unblinking eyes, "My name is Ian. I am your guide into the afterlife. A journey which will take us to some of the spookiest locations in the city. Some of them so terrifying, so blood curdling, that even the strongest of men has been known to weep in fear" - he glared for an uncomfortable moment at Paul, the tallest and biggest built of the rugby boys - "But first!" - people jumped again - "Hands up. Who here believes in ghosts?" He raised an eyebrow and looked around at the assembled group. About half had their hands in the air. That was normal. He smiled. "I can guarantee that by the end of the tour there will be more hands in the air." He rubbed his hands together and grinned, "If we are all ready, let us go to our first location. It just happens to be one of my favourites." He beckoned them all to follow. Ian stopped so abruptly only a few paces away that a few people bumped into each other. "Here we are." He said turning back to the group and spreading his arms. Some of the tour group laughed at the absurdity of the short walk. They were stood outside a franchise owned pub on the high-street. The lights and noise from inside were typical for a Friday night.

"Not being funny mate, be we had a drink here before

the match," called out Clive. Ian simply smiled and glared at the man.

"Ladies and gentlemen. May I present to you the Red Lion pub. Noted drinking spot of writers and actors. At least it was once. Now you can get a pitcher of blue stuff and a questionable burger for under ten pounds." The group chuckled among themselves. "What many people don't know is that this is one of the oldest building in the town. Built here when this whole place was just a small township in the marshes. Even before this was a public house, there was a boarding house for weary travellers to rest their heads on the long journey between London and Glasgow. Of course the building has been heavily built up since then, but there are still some pieces of the original wood work in the cellar. A kind word to the current landlord and you might even be allowed to see them. Although after hearing the rest of the story you might not want to see them. You see the first recorded owner, all the way back in the early fourteen hundreds, was a man by the name of Templeton. He would charge a small amount for people to stay at the inn. Most who stayed had a warm fire to ease their weary muscles and a good night's sleep. Most, but not all. For if you were travelling alone then this was not the place for you." He put his hands over his ears as signal to Clare. She covered her sons ears. "If Templeton took a shine to you he would drug your ale while you rested by the fire. Once incapacitated, he would drag you into the cellar and perform unspeakable acts. Your horse would also feed him for a time after. When a young girl escaped the cellar and ran into the street screaming, he was finally found out. The town's people found hundreds of human bones buried below the floor of the cellar. So many in fact that they couldn't remove them all and many still remain. They executed him by hanging him from his own rafters," Ian mimed the noose around his neck, "Some people say that his ghostly presence appears to those who visit the premises alone. I have also heard tales of ghostly screams when people go to the look at the wood in the cellar. Whatever you believe, just be careful when you drink your pitcher of blue stuff. You never know what Templeton might have in store for you," Ian smirked at the group.

"Eurgh!" Sam said with a shudder and cuddling under Julie's arm, "What a horrible man."

"I'd like to see him try anything with me," exclaimed Kathy, "I am a strong independent woman!" She snapped at the air. The hens were living up to their name by clucking laughter around her.

"Maybe that's what he likes," Said Paul winking at the hens, "I know I do." Ian, Julie and Simon all rolled their eyes in unison.

"Anyway," said Ian, pulling attention back to himself, "Let's head off to the next location and a tale of greed and corruption." Ian turned and started walking. The high-street grew quieter as they walked into a less commercial area.

"Excuse me Ian," Sharon had skipped forward clutching her purse to walk alongside the guide. He gave her a sideways look and carried on walking.

"Yes?" he asked.

"I was just wondering what your thoughts were on why some departed souls linger about whilst others... I don't know, move on? Am I saying that right?" She looked like a little mouse among the group.

"Well maybe we can open that one up to everyone since we're at the next location." He stopped abruptly again causing a few people to once again bump into each other.

"You really need to stop doing that," Kathy called out, "Sharon, give me a ciggie." Sharon fished a pack of twenty B&H gold and a lighter from her purse and handed them to Kathy.

"Do you need your phone too?" Sharon was rummaging.

"No. Just take these and don't lose them," She pushed the box of cigarettes and the pink clipper lighter back into Kathy's purse, nearly knocking the worn brown leather bag out of her hands.

"Ahem!" Ian stood with his back to a low rough stone wall. Behind that were lines of gravestones disappearing into the darkness as they receded from the orange light of the street lamps. In the centre of the darkness, surrounded by tall trees but partially illuminated by warm spotlights, was a rather delightful church. "Ladies and gentlemen, welcome to the church of Saint Christopher."

"How pretty," said Claire, "Don't you think?" She nudged Simon.

"Yeah its alright I suppose. Seen one church you seen them all though in my opinion," he said.

"Agreed," chimed in Julie.

"So what's so special about this one then?" called out either John or Paul. They were stood at the back and Ian couldn't fully see. There was a flash of blue light from the street some way off. Seeing a bench close by, Ian stood on it to address the group.

"Maybe we should answer Sharon's question first. Why do some spirits linger on this plane of existence? Any ideas? Hands up, don't be shy." One of the hens held up a hand. The one who had removed her sash and whistle. "Yes?"

"Innit like unfinished business or summit?" She had a thick Essex accent. "Ya know like, if I died right, I'd be well pissed off. And I'd like stay around to make sure my Darren don't get with any other birds. Ya know what I mean?"

"Interesting way to put it," said Ian, "Yes Sam." He pointed at her hand in the air.

"Well Buddhists believe that we enter what's called a bardo state, a kind of in-between place to wait until we're reborn. I always thought that was a rather lovely thought."

"My grandmother told me stories from her Jamaican roots when I was growing up. She believed that people had two souls, a good soul and an earthly soul. When someone dies the good soul goes to heaven and judgement but the earthly soul stays to guard the body for three days. If the proper precautions are not taken with the body though, the earthly soul can become a duppy, which is a bad ghost," explained Julie.

"What a load of bullshit!" called Paul. Ian could see it was definitely Paul.

"Steady on," said Simon covering little Johns ears.

"Sorry mate. It's just that when you die, that's it, you're dead. Worm food. Maggot fodder. Pushing up the daisies. Ghosts are just scary stories to spook kids into doing what they're told."

"And here in lies our quandary," Ian said in that practised theatrical voice, "There are so many theories that no one really knows. But one thing I do know for certain, is that this site was originally the site of pagan worship. Long before the church was built, there was a ring of standing stones. Many tales were told in the seventeen hundreds of witches who would gather under the light of the full moon and dance naked while making sacrifices to Lucifer himself. Mwahahaha." The over the top comedy villain laughter brought a smile to most faces. "The fact is it was all rubbish. There really was a set of standing stones here and I'm sure there were even witches that came here, but the truth is much more sinister. You see this land was also the site of a profitable mill. If you look at the road sign there you'll see it says Mill lane, not Church lane as is so often the case. The man who owned the mill lived there with his mother, his wife and five daughters. Just himself and seven women, I can't even imagine'" Several people laughed' "But you see there also lived close by a man named Batholomew Harper who owned another mill and coveted this one. He wanted to own both and so had offered to buy it, but the miller refused. Harper was not happy as you can imagine and came up with a plan. He had a brother who was the vicar of a parish a few towns over. Together they hatched a plot. Harper, the miller, wrote an anonymous letter to the clergy declaring witchcraft and blaming the poor family. Harper the vicar was dispatched to investigate. Once here they terrorised and tortured not only the family but anyone else whom Harper the miller may have had reason to get out of the way." Ian made the ear covering sign to Claire and waited for John's ears to be covered, "In total, the brothers executed twenty six people by burning them alive on this very patch of land. They had the church built to consecrate the land and wipe away the history of what they had done. Harper the miller lived to a ripe old age and managed many mills including the one behind this church. However, it is said that Harper the vicar was so repentant in his latter days that he jumped from the spire in guilt. There are others though that say he was pushed by a spectre in a black robe. Since then, the same figure has been recorded through history walking around the churchyard. So what do you think. Is it the vengeful spirit of the mill owner looking for his family? Or is it the ghost of the vicar, doomed for all eternity for his earthly sins? I'll leave that to you." His words hung in the air. He clapped loudly and smiled.,"Lets go. Time waits for no man and our next location is more than meets the eye." He jumped down from the bench and walked at a good pace down a road of Victorian fronted brick houses.

"So what made you decide on a ghost tour for your hen party luv?" John had slowed to walk beside Kathy and her girls.

"Wasn't my idea," She said as her heels clipped and clapped down the road, "Sharon thought it would be a fun thing to do while we waited for the club to open. So being maid of honour," she leaned to whisper to John, "Not my idea. It was my mums. You know" - she rolled her eyes - "So being maid of honour, the designated driver and tea total it seemed only fair to entertain her idea. What made you decide to follow a creepy man around in

184

the dark?"

"Dunno," John said, "Just kind of happened."

"Same here," Said Sam, "We decided to call it a day since we've been riding all day. Thought we'd look around for a little bed and breakfast or something, and well, here we are."

"What about you guys?" Julie asked Simon.

"We were driving to my mum's and saw the sign. Its not really the kind of things we usually do."

"And we're here." Ian stood in front of one of the houses. It looked like every other bay windowed facade on the street. They could see through the crack in the curtains that a light was on inside.

"Not exactly what you'd call spooky is it." Kathy was lighting another cigarette. "Don't tell us, you moonlight as an estate agent and this is an offer we'd be crazy to walk away from." The hens giggled around their leader. Except Sharon, who looked mortified.

"Nothing like that," Ian assured them, "Does anyone here know the name Jane Nottingham?" he looked around at the puzzled faces. It seemed fewer and fewer people remembered as time went on.

"It rings a bell," said Sharon, "But I can't quite place why."

"Same here," said Claire.

"Well then, let me tell you." He positioned himself with the house behind him and motioned for them all to gather round. They formed a neat little semicircle on the pavement facing the house. "Let me take you back to a time long ago when flower power was all the rage and rock and roll ruled the radio waves. That's right, the

1960's. Make that 1963 to be precise. The Beatles were riding high on their first number one hit 'From Me To You' and this part of the country was much like any other. All except for this house. This ordinary house on an ordinary street. That was until the Nottingham family moved it. Margery Nottingham was the widowed mother of three children. Kate the eldest, Mark the youngest and of course Jane in the middle. Jane was just twelve years old when they moved in to this house. A strange and quiet child. It was said that she didn't cry at her father's funeral but had withdrawn from the world since he passed. Margery had her hands full with Mark who was constantly being brought home by the local policeman for this and that. Nothing serious, but enough to keep her attention elsewhere as strange things started to happen around Jane. She told her sister that in the middle of the night she would wake up and see a shadow on the wall of a person, but there was no person there to cast a shadow. She said that she could feel it breathing near her in the night. Kate was understandably concerned about this and told her mum. Margery though, being a good Catholic woman, didn't believe them. It was only when Kate also started seeing this strange apparition in the night that Margery hung large wooden crosses over the doorways in each room. However, the household only had three night's peace before all hell broke loose." He grinned at the crowd and rubbed his hands together. He cupped his hands over his ears at Claire. "There are varying accounts of what happened that night but one thing is for certain. The disturbance was so bad that the police had to be called. Several neighbours came out into the street that night to witness what was going on. Some said that they could see the family members levitating inside, as the curtains thrashed back and forth and the lights flashed. Others said that the shadow of a man was dragging Jane up a wall by her hair. There was even a claim that lightning struck the house. Whatever happened, the screaming and shouting was enough to draw attention. When police arrived later, the house was dark and quiet. Margery and her children were sat just over there outside that house, wrapped in a neighbour's blankets and drinking tea. The official police report stated that all four family members were covered in small cuts and scratches which had been attributed to the huge amount of broken glass. You see every window of the house had been shattered from the outside in. There were also no signs of any crosses in the house; they had all simply disappeared. The police report did include something unexpected though. It read 'When entering the house, several officers heard a deep and trembling laughter from the upstairs. Upon inspection, no cause could be found as the house was empty.' Well this caught the attention of a group of psychical researchers. They practically moved in with the family, offering to pay for all the building repairs if they could run experiments. Margery, being a widow and only able to work part time, jumped at the offer. For three years they studied the family. Kate move out as soon as she was able, hating the attention. Mark turned from petty crimes to more serious ones and ended up in juvenile detention. All the studies then focused on Jane. They poked and prodded her. They shaved her head to monitor her brain waves meaning she had to wear a wig. They tied her up at night so she couldn't run away from the shadows that scared her so badly. Was it worth it? I'm sure the researchers thought so at the time. They had recordings of voices that came from nowhere. Pictures of objects levitating in mid air. They even had grainy videos of shadows moving in the night as Jane screamed to be let out. They eventually submitted their research at Cambridge University where an ethics committee accused them of torturing the girl and fabricating evidence."

"What happened to Jane?" asked Sam.

"I'm glad you ask. You see Jane went to a psychiatric facility for several months following the Cambridge committee's decision. Even though she still claimed to be tormented by spirits, they found her to be of sound mind and body. And so she came home. To this very house. Where she still lives to this day." He took a step to the side and motioned to the house. A ripple of gasps passed through the crowd and Ian looked to see the scared eye of a woman looking at them through the crack in the curtain. A shadow passed behind her and the curtains were snapped closed. "Well I think we've outstayed our welcome. Follow me." He lead the group away.

Ian was happy that both the hens and the rugby guys seemed to have sobered up. Whether it was from the cold night air, or the shock at the Nottingham house, he didn't mind. He pulled out the pocket watch by its chain and glanced down at the dial. 'Nearly finished' he thought.

"Looks like we might need to take a detour," called out Simon pointing to the blue flashing lights ahead of them as they headed back to the high-street. Ian continued on.

"No can do I'm afraid," he called back. They were

nearing the end of the road and about to turn onto the high-street when Ian stopped short and turned back to them. "Ladies and gentlemen. At the start of this tour I asked how many of you believed in ghosts. I also guarantee that by the end of the tour more of you would believe. And so we arrive at the last stop." People looked around trying to see further into the road ahead but Ian was blocking their view. Beyond the building society one side and the betting shop on the other, all they could see were parked cars and blue lights flashing. "Every town in Britain has a high-street," Ian announced, "That main road bustling with different people and shops of all kinds." It was now that the group started to realise there were no people around. It wasn't so late that the street would be deserted, but there was nothing. "This high-street here was the scene of a tragic accident not so long ago. Victims of fate in the form of an ordinary cork." Ian held up his hand to show a champagne cork between his fingers. "Such a small thing, an insignificant item. But when a soon to be bride accidentally caused it to explode from the bottle, it hit their designated driver in the back of head knocking her unconscious and causing the minivan they were all in the veer into oncoming traffic." The group started muttering among themselves as Ian turned his back on them and walked into the street still talking to them. "The young father tried to swerve to protect his wife and child, but they were sent skidding into the motorbike, unseating both riders. Of course more people might have survived if it wasn't for the drunk driver, celebrating a win with his friends, careening into them all instead of being able to brake." Ian stopped and looked down the street at the sight of the accident. A moment frozen in time. Police officers and paramedics like statues among the carnage. The lights on the vehicles flashing in rhythm.

"Is this some kind of joke?" Clive said walking up to Ian. "What is this, some sort of macabre theatre act?" He went to grab Ian but passed straight through him and landed with a thud on the floor behind him. The group started to panic and talked frantically among themselves. Some of them tearing up whilst other shook their heads.

"Ladies and gentlemen!" Ian's voice boomed and quietened the crowd. "Ladies and gentlemen," he repeated in a normal speaking tone, "Please calm yourselves and allow me to speak." A hush fell over them. "Thank you. As you are now painfully aware, you were all involved in an accident this evening. I'm afraid not all of you will survive. That is where I come in. It is my job to help you transition from one plane to the next," he pulled out the slip of paper, "If I call out your name, then I'm afraid I'm going to have to ask you to come and stand next to me. Understand?" They nodded amongst themselves. Still in shock, thought Ian. "Good. Sam, Kathy, Clive, Paul, Claire and little John." They slowly walked forward and went to stand with Ian.

"No!" Said Simon with tears in his eyes trying to hold on to Claire as she walked away.

"Please Simon. Hold on," Ian held up a hand to him. "Now, Hannah, Tammy, Natalie, you lucky hens, and you John, would you mind waiting at the side there," he pointed to the pavement. "And finally, Simon and Julie." He walked over to the two who were left in the middle and spoke in a soft comforting voice. "This group over here," he pointed to the group containing Claire, little John and Sam. "They are already dead."

"We're what?" shouted Clive. "What do you mean we're dead? I might pull through." Ian turned in frustration to the interrupting oaf.

"I very much doubt that. As much as medical science has advanced, there isn't much they can do to cure decapitation." Clive put a hand around his throat and went pale. "Now please be quiet." He took Simon and Julie both by the hand. "Those over there, they will live. They will wake up in some hospital not remembering any of this. But you two. You have a choice. You teeter between the living and the dead. The choice is yours."

"Go," said Sam stepping forwards with tears in her eyes.

"I can't," Julie sobbed back.

"Of course you can." Sam walked over and dried her wifes eyes with the edge of her sleeve. "This I my time to go, but it doesn't have to be yours. You can live a long and happy life. And when it is your time..." she lifted Julies chin to look into her eyes and smiled, "I'll be here waiting." They hugged and wept into each others arms.

"Simon?" Ian asked. Simon had not taken his eyes off if his wife and child. He walked over to them.

"There isn't a choice. I stay with my family, forever and always." He took Claire under his arm and kissed her on the top of the head. They both knelt down and pulled Little John into a big hug.

"Well there we have it. I'm afraid time is running short." Ian said looking at his watch in the blue glow of an ambulance light as it flashed. "Julie, if you wouldn't mind joining the others." Julie broke the embrace with Sam and joined the group on the pavement. "Who knows, maybe I'll see you again some day." Ian said as the group faded into nothing. He quickly turned round at the sound of heels on the street heading away form him.

"Kathy! Come back," shouted Sharon.

"I can't do it! I'm getting married!" Kathy called back as she rounded a corner and disappeared from view. Ian put his hand on Kathy's shoulder to stop her running after Sharon.

"Let her go. There's nothing we can do. Its time to pass over," Ian said, as behind him a glowing white corridor appeared.

"But what about Kathy? Where will she go?" Asked Claire.

"If she doesn't want to pass on, then she'll have to stay here. For a while at least. How else do you think ghosts are made?" said Ian as he stepped aside for them to walk into the corridor.

"What's through there?" Simon asked squeezing his son's shoulder. Ian shrugged.

"I honestly don't know. I'm just the ghost tour guide." He removed his top hat and bowed to them as they walked into the corridor. Once the last person had crossed the threshold it faded from the street. The world around him burst back into life and he walked away unseen by anyone and whistling to himself. "At least it didn't rain."

Printed in Great Britain
by Amazon

47722930R00111